IMPERFECT HEART

COMBAT HEARTS #4

TARINA DEATON

For my sister.
Who left me holding the cup.

ALSO BY TARINA DEATON

The Combat Hearts Series

Stitched Up Heart

Half-Broke Heart

Locked-Down Heart

Rescued Heart

Holiday Heart (only available to newsletter subscribers)

Coming Soon

The Jilted Duet

CHAPTER 1

"I'm going kill that damn trash panda."

The dumb animal chittered away at her from the high branch of the southern pine tree it had run up, still holding her keys.

Zoe Acevedo tromped around the side of the house, kicking at pine cones in her path. "I'm going to skin it and make a nice, fuzzy hat. Maybe Elba has room on her fancy cafe menu for raccoon stew."

She pulled her thick, curly hair—made even curlier by North Carolina's late summer humidity—back and twisted it up off her nape. The teeth had broken off the last of her clips and she hadn't had a chance to get more so she didn't have anything to keep it up. Letting it fall back down, she leaned into the open driver side window of her Honda CR-V and grabbed her cell phone from the console. Pulling up the contacts, she closed her eyes, inhaled deeply through her nose, exhaled slowly through her mouth, prayed for inner peace, and called her mother.

She answered on the first ring. *"Onde tu está?"*

"Olá, mamãe." The drive was fine. Thank you for asking."

"I talked to you an hour ago, why wouldn't the drive have been fine? Are you at the house?"

Zoe sighed. "*Sim*, I'm at the house. Where do you keep the hide-a-key?"

She stooped in front of the door and lifted the mat—nothing there. No flower pots or weird rocks around the porch either.

"Why do you need the hide-a-key? What's wrong with the keys I gave you?"

Zoe hung her head and pressed the palm of her hand against her eye socket. "A raccoon took my keys."

It sounded even more ridiculous saying it out loud.

"*Que?*"

"A raccoon. Fuzzy, gray animal. Looks like it's wearing a mask."

"I know what a raccoon is. How did it steal your keys?"

This was humiliating. "I unloaded my suitcases by the door and set the keys on top. I went to get a couple of boxes from the back of my car and when I turned around, the damn thing had my keys in his paws. When I shouted, he ran around the back of the house and up a tree."

Walking around the house while explaining the situation to her mother, she glared up into the tree the raccoon had climbed.

He was gone.

She kicked around the base of the tree, hoping the flea-ridden thief had dropped them. No such luck. Thankfully, it was only the house keys and not her car keys.

Her mother tsk-ed in her ear. "The neighbor has it, *querida*."

Zoe blew out a breath. "Which neighbor? Please don't tell me it's old lady Wilson."

"Zoe Mariana Olivera Acevedo, don't be disrespectful to your elders."

"*Sim, mamãe*." Zoe rolled her eyes. Old lady Wilson had been old and mean when she'd been in high school. There was no telling how much worse she was now.

"Tim has the key," her mother said.

"Who is Tim?"

"The police officer that moved next door a few years ago. I told you about him. He helped us when we had those horrible renters and your father had to evict them."

A vague memory surfaced of her mother telling her about that, but her mother was always telling her stories about people she didn't know, so she didn't always pay attention.

One of the many complaints her mother voiced. Along with not providing her with any grandchildren while Zoe'd had the chance and then divorcing her cheating ex, thereby ensuring her mother would never get any grandchildren from her. Because the five her brother and sister had supplied weren't enough.

"I'm so happy you're going to be living in the house and we won't have to worry about that anymore. Plus there's all the money we'll save by not having to pay a property manager."

"I'm just glad the timing worked out and you didn't have a renter." Because the prospect of living in a one-bedroom apartment, which was all she would have been able to afford, had not been appealing at all. "Which house does Tim live in?" she asked, walking around to the front.

"The Roberts house."

"All right. I'll call you back."

"We're headed on a shore excursion, so I won't have reception for a while."

"All right. I'll figure it out."

"*Tchau, caro.*"

"*Tchau, mamãe.*" She disconnected and slid the phone into her back pocket.

Back in front, she cut across the overgrown lawn to the two-story home that was a mirror image of her parent's house. She'd babysat for the Roberts family in high school. Hard to believe that was almost fifteen years ago.

Thirty-two wasn't by any means ancient, but the thought made her feel old.

A yawn forced its way out of her mouth, reminding her she'd been driving for ten hours and wanted nothing more than a hot shower and a bed. Neither of which she was going to be able to have without a key to the front door.

The empty driveway and dark house did not bode well for her chances. She pressed the doorbell anyway, hoping neighbor Tim's car was in the garage and he was a hard-of-hearing geriatric who went to bed at six o'clock every night.

A few minutes later, she had no such luck. Closing her eyes, she leaned her forehead against the door with a tired whimper. She'd leave a note on his door and nap in her car until he got home. Not ideal, but she was too tired to care.

Her phone rang and she answered it without raising her head or opening her eyes. "Hello?"

"Zoe, don't—"

She hung up. Pushing away from the door, she stared at the ornamental knocker.

"Baby Jesus hates me."

Her phone rang again and this time she looked at the display. She groaned. Her ex might actually have been preferable to her older sister.

"Hello."

"A raccoon?" Gabriella's laughter blasted from the phone.

Zoe waited for it to subside. "Did you call just to laugh at me?"

"Absolutely."

"I thought she was going on a shore excursion."

"She texted me and told me to check on you. Matthew, quit hitting your brother!"

"If you need to take care of that, I'll let you go," Zoe said.

"Ha. Ha. Normal occurrence around here. Did you get the key from the neighbor?"

"He's not home." She pushed away from the door and headed back across the lawn. "I don't suppose you have his number?"

"No. I think João has it."

"I'm not talking to João."

"Again?"

"He defended Mark."

"You didn't tell me that."

"I didn't want to rehash it."

Having her brother try to defend her ex for cheating on her had been almost as big of a betrayal as Mark cheating on her in the first place. Gabby had a tendency to try to play peacekeeper. She didn't need her trying to see João's side.

"Hmm. What are you going to do?" Gabby asked.

"Leave a note on the door and sleep in my car."

"That sucks. Too bad you can't sneak in the way we used to in high school."

"I couldn't climb that tree now even if it was still standing. And you did the sneaking." She opened the car door and rummaged in the console for a pen. "Too bad the latch on the kitchen window isn't still broken."

"I think it is."

She stood up. "Really? I thought dad fixed it years ago."

"It was one of those things he was going to get around to but never did and he didn't want to pay a handyman fifty dollars to fix it."

Yes! She might have a way in.

"I don't think you're going to fit through that window," Gabby said.

"What are you trying to say?"

"Uh, we're built like mom and your hips aren't going to fit through that window."

"I've lost fifteen pounds, I'll have you know. Divorce will do that to you."

She dragged the heavy-duty plastic trash can under the window.

"So really you lost two hundred pounds."

"Oh, yeah. Good one." She climbed on top of the bin. Sure enough, the latch was still broken.

"Have you heard from him since you left?"

"He's called a couple of times. I try not to answer. Hang on, I'm going to put you on speaker."

She slid the window open and assessed it. The trash can only put her almost waist-high to the bottom of the sill. There was no way to climb in sideways, which would be the easiest way in.

Okay, so it might be a tight squeeze. Normally she'd wait but she wanted to go to sleep. She'd hauled ass across the country, only stopping when she absolutely had to and waking up at the crack of dawn to get on the road. If she could get in the window, she'd be able to get a decent amount of sleep as opposed to the little she'd get in her car.

Gripping her phone, Zoe hefted herself into the window. Using her hips as a pivot, she leaned forward and wiggled in a little more, the metal track of the frame digging into the fleshy part of her hips.

"Well?" Gabby asked.

"Almost." She grunted. Her bruises were going to be epic in two or three days.

She tried wriggling in the rest of the way. With her feet in the air and all her weight forward, she didn't have any leverage. Shifting her weight to one side, she tried to roll onto her hip.

Nope. Nope. Nope. That hurt way too much to work and without being able to brace her feet and the heaviest part of her body on something, she'd never be able to crawl in.

Rolling back to her front, her head fell forward in defeat. "I'm not going to fit."

"I told you."

"Can we skip the *if-everyone-would-just-listen-to-me-in-the-first-place-everyone-would-be-so-much-happier* lecture right now?"

"As long as you know it's true."

"It's only true some of the time."

"Most of the time."

"Whatever."

If she hadn't been busy trying to rock her hips back out the window, she'd have told her sister where she could stuff her lecture.

The same predicament that kept her from going forward kept her from getting out. In her current position, she couldn't lower her legs enough to reach the trash can and kicking them didn't help. Neither did pushing against the backsplash under the window.

Puta merda. "Gabby."

"Yeah."

"I'm stuck."

CHAPTER 2

Tim Larken and his rookie trainee approached the apartment they'd been directed to for a possible domestic disturbance. Loud voices could be heard from inside. Tim nodded at Kevin, silently asking if he was ready, and knocked sharply on the door. The voices inside ceased.

A man in his mid- to late-twenties opened the door. He took one look at Tim and his partner and turned to the woman visible in the kitchen. "Seriously? You called the cops? I'm so fucking done with you."

The woman burst into loud sobs and covered her face.

"Sir, can I have you step outside please?" Tim posed it as a question, but it was more of an order. He stepped back, hand resting on his belt, close to his taser.

The guy shook his head and sighed. "Fuck this shit."

"Sir."

"Yeah, sure." He held his hands away from his body, palms opened.

Tim had a feeling this wasn't the guy's first run-in with the police, but the hair on the back of his neck told him something about the situation was off.

Another Haven Springs police cruiser pulled in front of the building and Chuck Martinez joined them in the front of the apartment.

"Officer Larken. Officer Moore."

"Officer Martinez," Tim said. Kevin nodded.

"Great. Now it's a party."

Tim gave his attention back to the guy they'd pulled from the apartment. "Do you have any ID on you?"

"In my back pocket."

"Go ahead," Tim said.

The guy sighed, pulled his wallet out, and handed over his driver's license.

Tim tilted the ID to see the print under the hologram. "Martin? This is expired."

Martin held out a military ID card. "Tennessee resident. They have a military exemption."

"Do you go by Martin?"

"Marty."

"All right, Marty. Why don't you tell us what the argument is about."

"I broke up with her. I'm trying to get my shit so I can leave. She wasn't supposed to be home, but called in sick just to fuck with me."

"Why would she do that?" Kevin asked.

He looked at Tim after he asked the question. Not sure what limits his previous field training officer had given him, Tim nodded shortly. Chuck tilted his head toward the apartment and left them to question the woman inside.

"Because she's crazy," Marty said. "I'm not talking the normal level of crazy you'd expect from a hot chick—she's certifiable."

He pulled down the collar of his shirt, exposing three red scratch marks. "She did this because I was messaging one of my buddies and making plans. She crawled into my lap and I thought cool, she's horny. No. Bitch dug her claws into my chest and told me when I was with her I needed to pay attention to only her."

He lifted the hem of his shirt to display a long bruise on his ribs. "This? Fucking metal vacuum tube because I didn't get the right kind of ice cream. She set my favorite boots on fire because my co-worker, who's a happily married grandmother by the way, answered my phone while I was with a client."

Chuck exited the apartment and joined them. "Your girl's got some pretty red marks on her face."

Marty held out his hands. "Not my girl anymore and I don't hit women."

"So you didn't put your hands on her?" Chuck asked.

"I pushed her away a couple of times while she was wailing on me, but I didn't shove her and I didn't hit her. Bitch deserved it, but my mama and sisters would tan my hide if I ever mistreated a woman."

Tim assessed Marty then shared a look with Chuck.

"Stay here," he told Marty.

Crossing his arms over his chest, he said, "Not going anywhere until I get my stuff."

They walked a few steps away.

"Do you believe him?" Kevin asked in a low voice.

"Not sure," Tim said. "Not a lot of guys would admit to getting beat on by a woman."

"Something's hinky," Chuck said. "But I'm not sure if it's him or her."

"Does she want to press charges?" Kevin asked.

"Nope," Chuck said. "She said she just wants him out of the apartment."

"Let's make that happen then," Tim said.

He walked back to Marty with Kevin while Chuck went back in the apartment.

"Here's the deal, Marty. She doesn't want to press charges, so we're going to make sure you get packed up and moved out."

Marty put his hands together like he was praying and looked heavenward. "Praise Jesus. Hallelujah. Thank you."

"Let's go." Tim tilted his head toward the open apartment door.

Marty beelined for the short hall, not looking at the woman still standing in the kitchen, and Chuck followed him.

The woman watched them, nervously chewing on a fingernail.

"Ma'am, can you please come out of the kitchen?" Tim asked.

She flinched, as if she wasn't expecting anyone to talk to her. "Sure. I was getting some water."

Something about her behavior seemed off. He'd unfortunately been on enough domestic violence calls to recognize micro signs of abuse and this girl's reactions felt forced.

"Is there somewhere you'd like to go while he packs?" Tim asked.

"Do I have to leave?" She sat down at the two-seater table.

"You don't have to."

"Is there someone you'd like to call to sit with you while you wait?" Kevin asked.

She peeked up at him through her lashes. "No. I'm okay."

Tim glanced at Chuck, who mouthed, "Hinky."

Yeah. Hinky was a good word for it. "Kevin? I'm going to step out and call this in."

Kevin nodded once. "I'm good."

Tim asked for the woman's driver's license and she pulled it from the purse on the table. Stepping into the doorway of the apartment, he kept an eye on the group inside. The call to dispatch only took a few minutes and when he returned inside, the girl, Ashley, was smiling up at Kevin and tucking a strand of hair behind her ear as she took a business card from him. Hopefully it was one of the abuse hotline cards they carried and not his own.

Tim headed to the bedroom and leaned against the jamb.

"Marty, you forgot to mention the assault charge."

Marty turned from the bed where he was stuffing clothes into a duffle bag. "Man, that was four years ago. Asshole put his hands on my kid sister."

"So you were defending her honor?"

"Told you I don't get off on mistreating women." He zipped the bag and hefted it over his shoulder then leaned down to grab the handle of a suitcase on the floor.

"Can I go?"

"Yeah, you can go," Tim said.

He gave a nod and shouldered out of the room, leaving the apartment in silence. A door slam and engine rev later, he was gone.

"Now what?" Ashley asked.

"Unless you want to file a report, we get out of your hair," Tim said.

"Oh, no." She shook her head, sending her hair over her shoulder only to flip it back. "I just never want to see him again. I have the worst luck with guys." She giggled and glanced at Kevin.

"Don't hesitate to call if he bothers you again," Kevin said.

Only his years of professionalism kept Tim from sighing. Kevin was new enough to the force to still have a hero complex. Tim had learned a long time ago most women weren't looking for a hero.

On the way back to their cruisers, Chuck stopped him with a hand on his arm. "You gonna talk to him about that?" He crooked his head at the closed door of the apartment.

"Yeah."

"You headed back to the station?"

Tim checked his watch. "We've got about thirty minutes left on shift. Why?"

Chuck grinned. "No reason really. Wondering if you were going to have the rookie type up the report."

Tim smirked. "What's the point of being an FTO if I can't pass off the paperwork to the trainee?"

"You know I can hear you, right?" Kevin asked from behind them.

Chuck looked over his shoulder. "So? Be glad Chief put the kibosh on glitter bombs. McCain had to shave his beard to get rid of it all. He looked like a stripper-fairy had ridden his face."

Tim grimaced. "Chief banned them because that shit got everywhere. The whole damn department sparkled for weeks."

"It did help arresting a couple of potheads, though."

"How's that?" Kevin asked.

"They got distracted by the 'ooh, shiny.'" Tim wiggled his fingers. "They thought we were taking them to a rave."

Chuck laughed and slapped Kevin on the back. "So be glad the only thing you get is paperwork."

He broke off to his car. "You playing softball Saturday?" he called.

"That's the plan," Tim said. As he opened the car door, the hair on the back of his neck stood on end and he turned to look at the apartment. A gap in the blinds closed. He slid into the car, keeping an eye on the apartment until Kevin pulled away from the curb.

"What number did you give her?"

"What do you mean?" Kevin asked.

"On the business card. Office or cell?"

"Both." Kevin pulled into traffic, heading back to the station for shift change.

Tim scrubbed a hand over his face, rubbing a the five-o'clock shadow that always appeared around noon.

"I get it—the desire to help and save everyone. It's why we do what we do. Or it should be why you do what we do, but getting involved with people you meet on the job is a bad idea."

"I didn't ask her out on a date. I gave her my card and told her to call if she had any problems."

"So you give her your office number, the non-emergency number, or the number to the abuse hotline, but you don't hand out your personal info."

"I'm trying to help. Isn't that what we're supposed to do? She just looked lost. I felt bad for her."

Kevin was getting defensive.

"Look, I was like you once—thought I could save the world."

He paused, deciding on the abridged version. "I met my wife on the job. Got a call, very similar to that one, felt the same way. I didn't set out to get involved—I was only trying to get her out of a bad situation. The more she depended on me, the more I wanted to be her knight in shining armor. Six months into our marriage she told me I was smothering her and filed for divorce."

There was more to the story, but Kevin didn't need all the gory details. Only the cautionary tale.

"That sucks, man."

"It does. All I'm trying to do is help you not make the same mistakes I made. I'm not the first cop to get personally involved with the job and I won't be the last, but I've never heard of one of those stories ending in happily ever after."

CHAPTER 3

Tim grabbed his bag from the passenger side of his truck and slammed the door. His cell phone rang as he unlocked the front door. He didn't recognize the number.

"Tim Larken." He shouldered open the door.

"Hi. This is Gabriella Carter. I'm Mariana Acevedo's daughter."

He dropped his bag inside the door and closed it. "Hi, Gabriella. Is your mom all right?"

"Oh, yes. Unless she's been kidnapped by pirates in Borneo in the last few minutes, I'm assuming she's fine."

What? "Oh-kay. What can I help you with then?"

"It's about the house—"

His phone beeped and he glanced at it. Seeing Mrs. Wilson's number, he asked, "Can you hang on a second?"

"But—"

He switched over to the other line. "Good evening, Mrs. Wilson. How is everything?" He worried about his older neighbor across the street. She was cantankerous and called him about every little inconvenience, but he knew she was lonely. Her kids lived on the west coast and rarely visited her. Being close to his own family, he tried to help out where he could.

"Timothy, someone is breaking into the Acevedo house."

That couldn't be a coincidence. He walked through the kitchen to the sliding back door.

"Why do you say that, Mrs. Wilson?"

"I saw someone skulking around earlier. They disappeared around the back of the house and I haven't seen them since."

If anyone would have noticed a potential break-in, it would be Geraldine Wilson. She was a one-woman neighborhood watch.

"I'll check it out, Mrs. Wilson." He disconnected and headed across the shared lawn. Sure enough, a pair of shapely legs stuck out of the kitchen window.

The bottom the legs were attached to was just as shapely. He understood the owner's predicament—her legs were too short to reach the garbage can she'd obviously used to boost herself up.

Just as he drew close to the potential burglar, his phone rang loudly. A shriek came from the other side of the window and her legs flailed wildly. He dodged out of striking distance and answered.

"Tim, it's Gabby. I think we got cut off."

Shit. He'd forgotten to switch back over to the other line. "Sorry about that. Is this about a pair of legs sticking out of your parents' kitchen window?"

"Gabby! Who are you talking to?"

The question echoed from the disembodied legs and the phone.

"Sorry," Gabby said. "I've got you on three-way."

This was not the situation he'd always fantasized about when it came to a three-way. He shook his head at how quickly his mind went X-rated. "No problem. I'm guessing you know who the legs belong to."

"My sister, Zoe. She got locked out. I told her she wouldn't fit and she should wait until you got home, but she wouldn't listen."

Zoe's feet kicked again. "You're the least favorite daughter."

Tim smiled and covered his mouth with his hand to keep from

laughing out loud. This had to be one of the more ridiculous things he'd ever encountered and he'd once had to wrestle a greased-up frat boy to the ground during pledge week at the University of North Carolina.

"I've got it," he said. "She'll call you back when she's loose."

The sisters spoke rapid-fire in a language he didn't understand. It wasn't Spanish. He knew Mrs. Acevedo was Brazilian, so maybe Portuguese?

He shoved his phone in his pocket and tried to figure out the best way to get Legs out of the window. Even at six-foot-five, he didn't have the leverage to lift her hips from the window, never mind the room for his hands.

Pulling the trash can to the side, he looked in the window. "Zoe?"

"Yeah?" A mass of dark curls turned, trying to see over her shoulder.

"I'm Tim, your neighbor. How're you doing?"

"My ass is wedged in a window, all the blood is rushing to my head, and I'm going to have this window frame permanently imprinted in my hips. Otherwise, *perfeito*."

He chuckled softly at her dry tone. "Got it. Well, there's no easy way to do this so, sorry for any awkwardness from this point forward."

"Because this isn't awkward enough already?"

She might have a point. He turned his back to the wall and bent at the knees. Leaning sideways, he maneuvered his shoulder under her thighs and stood.

She yelped as her weight was lifted from the frame.

"Okay, I'm going to walk forward slowly. Use your hands to hold your weight up and let me know when you're almost clear of the frame so I don't drop you on your head."

"Okay."

Shuffling forward slowly, he moved away from the wall of the house.

"Wait!"

He stopped. "What's wrong?"

"My hair's caught."

"Where?"

"On the frame."

"Can you get it?"

"I can't hold myself up and untangle my hair."

"Are you out of the window?"

"Mostly."

"Okay. I'm going to back up and hold you up. See if you can get it uncaught."

"All right."

He backed up slowly, lowering her part way down his body until her waist was on his shoulder instead of her hips. He felt the wall at his back and stopped. "Is this good enough?"

"I think so. Hang on."

Her weight shifted on his shoulder as her torso lifted behind him. Her firm breast pressed against the side of his face. Now that he was standing still and not worried about pulling her from the window, he realized both of his hands gripped her round ass. He was pretty sure his pinky has slipped under the edge of her jean shorts.

Little Tim decided to pick that moment to realize he held a lush woman in his arms with equally lush parts of her pressed against him.

"Got it!"

Distracted and unprepared for the sudden shift of her body weight as she raised her upper half, he stepped to the side to try to regain his balance and knocked into the garbage can. His foot twisted when it made contact with the side of the receptacle instead of the ground and he lost his balance. Knowing he was going down, he tried to twist so he didn't land on top of Zoe.

They fell in a tangle of limbs and he ended up on his back with a face full of cleavage. She pushed up, giving him a clear view down the v-neck of her t-shirt and the black, lacy bra that appeared more for show than functionality as the tops of her tits were spilling over the edge.

"I'm so sor— Come here, you stupid vermin!"

She lunged up, landing a knee dead center of his crotch and an elbow to the side of his temple.

He rolled to his side with a groan, clutching his dick, staring after a crazy woman chasing a raccoon.

SHE DIDN'T CATCH the raccoon, but she did find where it had dropped her keys. Stupid trash panda. Mumbling to herself on the way back to the man she'd...unmanned...she couldn't come up with a sufficient apology.

Thanks for getting me unstuck, sorry I kneed your junk. If the bookstore failed, she could always start a line of apology cards.

As she got closer, she realized he was in uniform. "Well, shit. I assaulted a cop. Could this day get any worse?" She looked up at the sky. "Don't answer that."

Squatting next to Tim, she asked, "Are you okay?"

"Yup," he grunted.

"Sorry I abused your...you know."

"'S okay. Pretty sure it's karma."

He sat up and she got a good look at him. *E um gato sarado. Que lindo!* Gabby had obviously never met Tim or she would have gushed about how good looking he was. A five-o'clock shadow with a hint of gray at the edge of his sculpted jaw showcased a full bottom lip. Speechlessness struck when he blinked watery, gray-green eyes at her.

She pulled her lips between her teeth to make sure she wasn't gaping at him and tried to think of something intelligent to say.

"You punch a lot of guys in the family jewels?" Yup. Intelligent. She should send MENSA an application.

"No. Worse." He pushed himself up and stood slowly. "Made fun of my brother when it happened to him."

She stood as well. Whoa, he was tall. She barely reached his shoulders and had to crane her neck to look up at him.

"Oh." She held out her hand. "Zoe."

Remembering the keys she'd found and looped middle finger through, she pulled back her hand before he could shake it.

"I found my keys. A raccoon took them and ran off. I tried to find the hide-a-key, but it wasn't there. Otherwise I would have just used that instead of trying to climb in the window."

"I made your parents get rid of it," he said.

Distracted by the movement of his lips, she lost track of what they were talking about. "Get rid of what?"

"The hide-a-key."

"Why?"

"Because it's not safe and it invites people to break in."

"Who would break into a house next door to a cop?"

His eyebrows rose and he looked at the window, then back at her.

She felt the flush rise up her neck. "Well, I forgot you were a cop."

"Would remembering have stopped you from trying to crawl through the window?" he asked.

She cocked her head an considered his question. "No. And it wasn't like I was actually breaking in. It's my house. Well, my parents' house, but I live here now. Besides, I'd just driven for ten hours. I wanted to get in and unpack."

When would the word vomit stop?

He crossed his arms. "How'd that work out for you?"

Her brows pinched together. "You and my sister. No one likes a know-it-all."

He dropped his arms. "A know— I'm merely pointing out that had you waited, you'd be in the house at the same time without

22

any damage to either of our dignities. Or, if you had called, I could have come home earlier and let you in."

"I didn't have your number." Enough chit-chat. She was tired and wanted to blow up her air mattress so she could go to sleep. Walking around his hulking body that filled out his uniform a little too well, she beelined for the front of the house.

"Your sister had it," he said from behind her.

"No. João had it."

"Your brother?"

She stomped passed the suitcases and boxes. "Yes."

"Why couldn't you have called your brother?"

"I'm not talking to him at the moment."

"Why aren't you talking to him?

Pausing with the key in her hand, she said, "I don't remember. I'm sure I have a reason." Lying to a police officer didn't feel all that great, but she didn't want to get into the screwed-up relationship between her and João.

"A good enough reason to get stuck in a window instead of calling him to get my number?"

Spinning around, she was confronted by his amused face. She fumed. He was worse than her sister. He was just like her brother. Stupid condescending *machismo*. He was probably married to a stick-figure supermodel and had beautiful children who modeled for Pottery Barn Kids.

"Look. Thanks for your help. It was suitably awkward. Have a nice night."

Turning the door handle, she spun and smacked her face on the still closed door.

He cleared his throat behind her. "Deadbolt."

"Yup." Lacking all grace and coordination, it took three tries to finally get the door open. She stormed through and slammed it behind her. Leaning back against it, she closed her eyes.

"You need any help with these boxes?" His voice carried through the door.

"I'll get them after I pee!" She scrunched up her face. *Oh my god!*

What was wrong with her? She was a thirty-two-year-old divorced woman getting ready to open her own successful-if-she-died-trying business.

Sleep deprivation. That had to be the reason for all the babbling and awkwardness. That and he was the most beautiful man she'd ever laid eyes on and she hadn't missed the fact that his eyes had strayed down her top or that his warm breath had raised goosebumps on the sensitive skin of her breasts.

"Suit yourself."

She banged the back of her head against the door. "Baby Jesus hates me."

CHAPTER 4

Z oe stood in the midst of her life, packed and sorted into forty-eight moving boxes, and stared at the poster-sized to-do list tacked to the wall of her dining room.

Household goods delivery was checked off. That was the easy part. Unpacking was the part that sucked. Every move she wondered if it would be easier to sell everything at one assignment and buy new at the next. Definitely not less expensive, but how much was a stress-free life worth nowadays?

"More money than you have." She clapped her hands, trying to motivate herself. "All right. Everything's easier with a list. A list is a roadmap to a goal."

She tore off a blank sheet of self-stick easel paper and stuck it to the wall next to the other list. Grabbing her trusty marker, she wrote down the order of the rooms to be unpacked. Kitchen definitely needed to be first so she could find her wine and shot glasses, then her bedroom so she could sleep in her own bed tonight. She'd washed and vacuum sealed her bedding before she'd left Arizona so all she had to do was unpack it and make her bed. They wouldn't be dryer fresh, but they'd be damn near close enough.

The doorbell rang as she cut open the first box. She smiled when she saw who was on the other side of the peephole.

Elba wrapped her in a tight hug as soon as she opened the door.

"You're here. You're really here."

Zoe laughed, hugging her back. "Where else would I be?"

"I don't know." She let her go and stooped to pick up the cloth grocery bags at her feet, following Zoe into the house. "Somewhere changing your mind?"

"Nope. I'm here. This is happening."

"Okay." She closed her eyes, touched her middle fingers and thumbs together as if she was meditating and blew out a breath.

"I got a little nervous this afternoon when they blocked off part of the cafe to knock a huge hole in the wall."

Zoe's eyes widened and she grinned. "Shit's getting real."

Elba mirrored her grin. "Shit is most definitely getting real." She squealed and did a little shimmy. "I brought sustenance and wine."

"Mmm. What did you bring?"

She held out one of the bags. "A light, spring salad and a simple quiche lorraine."

Zoe took the proffered bag. "*Simples, meu traseiro.*"

"What's that mean?"

She smiled. "Simple, my ass."

Elba gave her another impromptu hug. "Oh, I've missed you."

"I've missed you too. I can't believe it's been almost ten years." Zoe led the way to the kitchen and set the bags on the counter.

"Do you want to eat first and then help me unpack or start unpacking and then eat?"

Elba looked at her blank wrist. "Oh gosh, would you look at the time?"

"Elba…"

"I'm kidding. Let's eat while it's still warm. If I stop in the middle of unpacking, I won't want to start again."

Grabbing paper plates and plastic utensils, Zoe cut a slice of quiche. "What's in the other bag?"

"Lubricant."

"KY or Castrol?"

Elba threw her head back and laughed. "Margaritas."

"Well, in that case, let me get my very best stemware."

Zoe set her plate on the counter and grabbed two plastic cups while Elba pulled the large thermos out of the other bag.

"Do you serve cocktails at the cafe?" Zoe asked.

Elba shook her head. "I was putting the paperwork together for a beer and wine license, but I'm waiting until the hole is done."

"Why?" Zoe took the cup Elba held out to her.

"I have to submit a floor plan and it's easier to do that once than it is to file and then resubmit."

"Shit. I'm sorry. You should have said something." Guilt that she'd delayed her friend's expansion goals landed in her stomach like sour milk.

"What are you sorry for?" Elba indicated over her shoulder with a thumb. "I figured as soon as I told you all the ideas I have, you'd have at least thirteen lists made."

Zoe took a bite of quiche. "What do you have planned?"

"I was going to wait until you'd had a chance to settle in, but since you asked… The first thing I want to do is expand into dinner service, but it means hiring another chef. Then, I want to partner with local wineries to do a monthly menu tasting paired with their locally produced wine. Advertise it as very exclusive and then have bottles of their wine available at the cafe. I also want to do a monthly wine and books event. Kind of like a book club, but where you invite authors to come in and meet their readers in a relaxed setting. Again, intimate and exclusive.

Zoe tried to blink away the sting in her eyes.

"What?" Elba sat up straight in her chair. "Is it too much? We don't have to do the book thing if you have other ideas."

"No." She shook her head. "I love it. It's just— After everything that's happened over the past nine months, it's fan-freaking-tastic to finally talk to someone that gets it and doesn't think I'm crazy."

"Oh, honey." Elba set her plate down and pulled Zoe into another hug. "Of course I think you're crazy. But I also think you're passionate and determined and can accomplish anything you set your mind to."

Zoe took comfort from her friend's easy affection. "I don't know what I'm going to do if this fails."

"Hey." She pushed her away and gripped her shoulders. "This is not going to fail. It's an awesome idea and I saw your business plan. It's genius. Plus, you have a list."

Zoe laughed. "It's easier to visualize when there's a list."

"I know." She patted her shoulder and let her go. "I'm a little surprised you only have two up on the wall."

"I have another one ready to put up in the office. And one in my planner. And a calendar with a separate timeline."

She wiped away a tear she blamed on stress. If she admitted to anything else, the fear and uncertainty she'd so far managed to hold at bay might paralyze her.

Switching topics, she asked, "When do I get to meet my goddaughter again? The last time I saw her she couldn't even walk."

"Come by the café this weekend for lunch. She's started helping out for a few hours to earn some money."

Zoe sipped her drink. "Isn't that against child labor laws?"

"Possibly, but there aren't enough chimneys in North Carolina for her sweep so it was either putting her out to beg or putting her to work bussing tables." Elba grinned. "She asked to earn some money. I told her if she helped out in the café she could keep the tips."

"What does she need money for?" Zoe leaned against the counter.

"The Model U.N. club at her school is trying to raise money for a trip to New York to visit the actual U.N."

Zoe lowered her glass. "U.N. as in United Nations?"

"Yup." Elba over-pronounced the *p*.

"In North Carolina?"

"Yup. Guess whose idea it was to start the club?"

"April's?" Zoe asked with a grin.

"Ding. Ding. Ding. I swear that girl has her sights on being President one day. She's so smart and determined."

"Good for her."

"If I didn't know better, I'd say she was your spawn. That girl drives me to drink."

"Speaking of..." Zoe set her glass down and crossed the kitchen. Pulling a bag of lemons from the counter, she held them out to Elba.

She took them gingerly. "What's this?"

"Call me life."

"Huh?" Elba's look of confusion was almost comical.

"When all the shit started with Mark and I said 'fuck it,' I was trying to explain to a friend how I could make such an impromptu decision. I said, 'when life gives you lemons' and she said, 'do tequila shots?' She was trying to imply my decision was drastic and over the top, but I was like, yeah. Hell, yeah. Who the hell wants to go through life drinking freaking lemonade?"

She pulled a bottle of Patrón out of the freezer. "My plan for tonight was to do a couple of shots and start crossing things off my to-do list. Want to join me?"

Elba's eyes widened. "Oh hell no. I'll help you unpack, but I remember the last time we did tequila shots. I shouldn't—but I do."

Zoe took two red plastic cups from the stack on the counter, unscrewed the top on the bottle, and poured. "It wasn't that bad."

Elba handed the lemons to her. "I puked for twelve straight hours."

Cutting open the bag, she sliced a lemon into wedges on a

paper plate. "We were drinking cheap, crappy tequila. This is much better."

Holding out a wedge and a cup, she said, "One shot. Call it a celebratory drink to welcome me to North Carolina and the start of my new life."

Grumbling, Elba took the shot. "Only because I love you and missed you and am really happy you're here. Where's the salt?"

They both licked the backs of their hands and dusted them with salt.

Picking up a wedge of lemon, Elba held out her drink. "What are we drinking to?"

There was so much she could toast. To not being the perfect wife or daughter. To turning her back on everything that sucked the life from her soul. To everything she wanted to accomplish. To being on her own for the first time in her adult life with nothing but a dream and a to-do list.

She touched her cup to Elba's. "To new beginnings."

CHAPTER 5

Tim could hear faint music from the other side of the door when he rang the doorbell.

A minute later, the door swung open and a petite brunette stood in the doorway. With one hand on the door and the other on her hip, she looked him up and down in an appreciative way.

She looked over her shoulder and called out, "Hey, Zoe! Someone sent you a stripper-gram."

"What?"

Zoe turned the corner from the kitchen. Her eyes widened when she caught sight of him and her mouth parted, then closed again. A pretty blush colored her cheeks.

As embarrassing as it was to be confused with a stripper, although it wasn't the first time a woman had made that assumption of him when he knocked on a door in uniform, it was worth it to see Zoe's reaction.

He'd had a hard time keeping her out of his thoughts this past week. Teasing her and watching her get riled up and nervous and more riled up the more nervous she'd gotten had been amusing. When Mrs. Wilson called to inform him a moving truck had blocked the road for most of the day, he'd jumped at the chance to check on Zoe. Sure, he could have checked on her out of neighborly concern, especially since he'd watched over the house for her parents, but having an additional excuse hadn't hurt.

Zoe pulled her friend away from the door by the shoulders. "Elba, this is my neighbor Officer Larken."

"Tim is fine." He held out his hand.

She shook it with surprisingly firm grip. "Yes, you are. I'm Elba."

"Elba like—"

"No, not like elbow with an *a*," she said with a scowl.

"I was going to say like the island."

She turned to Zoe. "He's hot *and* smart. You should totally sleep with him."

"Oh my god." Zoe pushed her friend away from the door. "I apologize for my friend. She lost her filter in a tragic spelunking accident. Is there something I can help you with?"

"I received a call from one of the neighbors about a moving truck blocking the road. You were the only one I knew who had moved in lately, so I thought I'd stop by to see how you were settling in."

"It was only blocking half the road and it left hours ago. It was old lady Wilson, wasn't it? I can't believe she still has it out for me."

"Why would she have it out for you?" Elba asked.

"I shaved her cat when I was fifteen."

"You—what?"

Zoe sighed. "She used to have this long-haired Persian cat when I was in high school that she let run around outside. One summer I found the poor thing panting under some bushes trying to stay cool. So I took it to the groomer and had it shaved."

Elba cocked her head. "I can't imagine why an old lady would be mad that you shaved her pussy."

Tim swiped a hand over his mouth, unsuccessfully trying to hide a smile.

"I swear I told you that story," Zoe said.

"Oh no. No, no. I would have remembered a story about you shaving an old lady's pussy."

"Would you stop saying it that way?" Zoe swatted Elba's arm.

"Are you kidding? This is gold! I can't believe I've missed out on twelve years of teasing you about shaving an old lady's pussy." Elba bent at the waist, overcome with hilarity.

Tim had a hard time keeping a straight face. He was going to laugh about this for a good long while.

Zoe pulled her friend farther away from the door. "As you can see, I'm settling in and still have a lot of unpacking to do. Have a good night and please ignore any screams you may hear coming from the house. I'm going to watch a horror movie."

Tim stared at the closed door and finally let out the chuckle he'd been holding in. Walking across the yard between their houses, he pictured a younger Zoe struggling to hold down a squirming cat while she took a pair of clippers to it and laughed even harder. Bad sexual innuendos aside, it was a funny story.

In his bedroom, he removed his utility belt and changed his uniform for workout clothes. Taking his dry cleaning bag downstairs, he set it by the door so he'd remember to drop it off on the way to work in the morning.

The clock on the wall in the garage showed him stopping by Zoe's had put him fifteen minutes behind his routine—he was going to have to cut his run short to finish his workout in time to watch *Jeopardy!* Not that he was complaining, since it'd given him an excuse to talk to her again.

He scrolled through his phone for a playlist then docked it on the speakers. Cranking up the speed on his treadmill, he tried to determine what it was about Zoe that intrigued him so much even after only two brief encounters. Other than her gorgeous curves. He didn't know anyone who wouldn't consider them an asset, but it was more than that. There were plenty of women he'd met since his divorce with curves for days—something about Zoe set her apart. In the quick interactions he'd had with her, she'd been funny and sarcastic, bold and bashful.

She was a contradiction. For the first time in longer than he could remember, he was interested in a woman. Truthfully, and it had taken him a long time to come to terms with reality, he hadn't been interested in his wife. He'd felt protective. He'd convinced himself he'd been in love, but he'd never really wanted to know what made her tick.

He wanted to know what made Zoe tick.

He finished his workout and headed to the kitchen. Setting water on to boil, he plugged in the counter top grill and pulled out broccoli and marinated chicken breast from the refrigerator. It was simple and easy. He'd tried to keep up the complicated meals he'd made for his ex, but it had been too much food and took too much time. At least simple grilled chicken and steamed vegetables or a salad wasn't freezer meals. He wasn't so entrenched in his bachelorhood that he'd sunk that far.

His home phone rang and he picked it up without looking at the caller ID since there were only three people who would call him at home.

"Hello?"

"Hey. Are you working this weekend?" his brother, Jase, asked.

"I'm off Friday and Saturday. Why?"

"Bree wants to know if you'll meet us for lunch downtown."

He smiled at the mention of his soon-to-be sister-in-law. He hadn't been too sure of her and Jase's relationship at first given the circumstances of how they met, but his brother had come out of his self-imposed solitude and he knew it was because of Bree.

"Sure. When and where?"

"Saturday at the weekend market. She wants to ask you a question."

"Don't tell him that!" Bree said in the background.

"I can't take a dog." He threw broccoli into the steamer basket in the pot.

Bree and her friend Denise were always pestering him to adopt one of their rescue dogs, but his schedule wasn't conducive to taking care of one.

"Tim, it's Bree."

He lifted the lid off the grill and poked at the chicken. "Hi, Bree. I can't take a dog."

"Can you at least meet her first before you make a decision? She's old and lazy. You won't have to walk her or play with her. Just make sure she goes out a couple of times a day and has a cozy place to sleep at night."

He sighed. That sounded like the ideal life. Maybe if he gave in on the laziest dog in the world, they'd stop asking him every week. "All—"

"She just needs a place short-term until we can find her forever home. And that won't be long, she's really a sweetheart."

"All right."

"Really? You'll take her?"

"I'll meet her. We'll see how lazy she really is before I make a decision."

"Yay! Denise will bring her by Thursday after work. That way you'll have the weekend with her. Here's Jase."

"Man, you owe me. I bet her a back rub you were going to say no," Jase said.

"Sure, I'll rub Bree's back."

"You're going to keep your damn hands to yourself."

He smirked and pulled his chicken off the grill. "Then why'd you say I owed you?"

"I'm gonna make you rub my back."

"You'll have to wax it first."

"You wish you were this manly."

"I don't need that much fur to be manly. We still meeting this weekend since I agreed to take the dog?"

Jase repeated his question to Bree. "She said yes, that's not the only reason to see you. She likes you for some inexplicable reason."

"I'd say it's because she has good taste in men, but she's marrying you so it can't be that."

"Whatever asshole. Later."

"Later." He ended the call and set the phone back in the charger. Grabbing a beer from the fridge, he took his plate into the living room and turned on the television to catch the first round of *Jeopardy!*

Maybe a dog wouldn't be so bad. At least then he'd have someone to listen to him while he answered trivia questions.

TIM SET the wet dish in the drainer and shut off the water. Nine-thirty at night and he was headed to bed. Granted he woke at four a.m., but damn he felt old.

Leaving the light off, he crossed his bedroom, passing in front of the window. Movement in his peripheral made him stop, back up two steps, and look out the window.

Zoe was in her bedroom. Directly across from his. With only the sheers drawn. And she was dancing.

In nothing but a thin, strappy top and her underwear.

She was unpacking, moving between boxes on the bed and the closet, but she danced instead of walked. He couldn't hear the music, but the movement of her hips made him think something Latin or with a heavy drum beat.

He stepped closer to the window, bracing one hand on the frame.

He should step back. He should close his own curtains and let her know she should close hers. Instead, he watched. His gaze followed as she shimmied around the room. She rolled her hips and his cock tingled as blood rushed to it.

36

Fuck. This was wrong. It didn't stop him from rubbing the smooth fabric of his gym pants against his rock-hard dick.

She did some kind of spin and her arms rose above her head. He groaned and slipped his hand into his pants, gripping his shaft tightly. Damn, she was sensual. Her hips rolled and swayed. He rubbed his hand up and down in time to the shake of her hips.

It'd been over a year since he'd been in a serious relationship with anyone other than himself and his imagination ran wild. He wanted to dig his fingers into the soft flesh of her outer thighs while she ground down on his cock. Closing his eyes, he pictured her riding him, raising her hands to her mass of curls, throwing her head back as she cried out with pleasure.

What was he doing? He pulled his hands out of his pants and hung his head. He was a cop. Not only that, but he considered himself to be a pretty decent guy and he didn't take advantage of women. Even if it was only watching as they moved seductively around their bedroom. Especially when they were in their bedroom and unaware. If she ever wanted to do that while he watched, knowing he watched, that would be one thing, but he wasn't going to take the choice away from her.

Her light was still on, but he couldn't see Zoe. Had she seen him standing in the window, watching her like some creepy Peeping Tom?

Fuck. He closed his curtains, which he should have done instead of watching her like some horny teenager seeing his first pair of tits.

CHAPTER 6

Z oe stood across the street and stared at her future home. Well, her future bookstore, but she planned on spending most of her time there, so it would effectively be her home. Elba's cafe was on the left and an eclectic secondhand store was on the right. On the other side of Elba, a hair salon and day spa.

Located on a side road smack dab in the middle of Market Street and across from one of the most popular parking lots, they would get a lot of traffic on weekends. Even now, in the middle of the day, there were plenty of shoppers. The only way it would have been better was if it had been on Market Street.

Crossing the street, she pulled open the door and went in. Her heart pounded in her chest and she rested her palm over it. Until then, she'd only seen it in pictures.

It was chaos. Saws whirred. Hammers pounded. Looking at the mess, it was hard to picture what it would look like in four weeks. That was the deadline for completion she and the contractor had agreed to.

"Can I help you?" A man approached from the right, skirting a pile of wood.

"Hi. I'm looking for Linda."

He turned and shouted over the noise. "Linda! Someone here to see you!"

An older blond woman moved away from a large table made of a plywood board and saw horses and headed toward her. Even though she was average height for a woman, Zoe still felt small standing next to her.

A spark of recognition lit in her eyes as she drew closer. She held out her hand. "Zoe?"

"Yes." She shook the woman's hand, rough with calluses.

"It's nice to finally meet you in person. I'd hug you, but I'm probably covered in sawdust. How was your trip?"

"That's okay. Another time." Zoe smiled. They'd been virtually introduced by Zoe's Women in Small Business mentor and had never met in person. Even so, she and Linda had connected.

Linda had understood Zoe's vision and been able to put to paper what Zoe had only been able to verbalize. "The trip was good. Long. I drove almost non-stop for two and a half days."

"You settling in all right? Do you need any help with anything at the house?"

"No, thank you. I've got everything unpacked. I just need to find places for it all."

"I don't miss that part of the military. Glad I was finally able to put down roots in one place and not have to pick up anymore."

Zoe inhaled deeply. "That's the idea."

"Do you want to start at the back? The kids' corner is almost finished."

"Really? I thought you said it was going to be at least another week."

Linda tilted her head side to side. "I don't like to tell people I'm ahead of schedule until things are done. That way they don't have any expectations. Let me get you a cover." She walked over to the man who'd greeted Zoe and picked up a white hardhat.

Zoe took the hat and tried to squash it down over her curls. It sat precariously on her head and she wasn't sure how much protection it would afford if something dropped on her.

Skirting the edge of the large room, Linda led her to a space in the back free of tools.

Pointing up, she said, "This is the loft we talked about."

Zoe turned in a circle taking in the short, wide bookcases and the arched entry to the stairs up to the loft.

"Can I...?" She pointed to the steps.

"Go for it." Linda swept her arm out, inviting Zoe to explore.

She took off the hard hat and crouched through the opening, using her hands to help climb the short staircase through the low passage. This would have been so much fun when she was a kid. When she reached the top, the ceiling was still low enough she had to crouch but would be the perfect height for kids. One side of the wall was a silhouette of a castle, complete with a small turret kids could crawl into.

She looked through the portholes cut into the wall—big enough for a kid to poke their head out of, but small enough they couldn't fall through. In her mind she pictured them sprawled around the area reading on large bean bags while their parents shopped in the rest of the store. Reading had been her escape growing up. Having somewhere other than her closet to escape to would have been a dream. Giving that to kids, encouraging their imaginations and love of reading, had been a priority when she'd first contemplated opening a bookstore.

"My daughter is going to paint the details on the castle inside the loft," Linda called up. "She didn't want to start painting down here until she'd had a chance to talk to you."

Back at the bottom, she hugged Linda, sawdust and all. She'd given life to Zoe's dream. "Thank you."

Linda rubbed her back and patted it a couple of times. "I'm not even done showing you the rest of the store, yet."

"I don't care. It's perfect."

"Hey." Linda released her and held her at arm's length. "I have a rule: no crying on the job site unless you're bleeding."

Zoe laughed and rubbed her nose. "I'll try to not do anything that causes me to bleed."

"Good. Let me show you the solution we came up with for the doorway between the bookstore and the cafe."

Her stomach flipped. No matter how many drawings or schematics Linda had sent, Zoe hadn't been able to visualize the concept. Eventually she decided to trust Linda's expertise, but she'd been worried.

Linda stopped in front of a row of floor to almost-ceiling bookcases along the shared wall between the bookstore and Elba's cafe. Stepping on a doorstop at the base of the shelf, she released it. She reached into one of the shelves about shoulder height and pulled a lever, then bent and pulled another one. Moving to the bookcase beside it, she did the same, then swung the shelves out like a set of double doors, revealing the cafe on the other side of the wall.

Zoe covered her mouth with her hands as she spotted Elba behind the counter, then clasped her hands under her chin. "I love it."

Linda held the side of a shelf and grinned.

"Here, look." She pointed down. "There are door stops on either side and if you look at the top of the bookcase, there are security latches that secure it into the ceiling."

"So it has to be unlocked from both sides in order for it to be opened?" Zoe asked.

"Yes. I know security was a concern for both of you since you're independent businesses and are going to have different hours."

Elba joined them. "I was wondering how that was going to work. I left one day and there was a hole and a tarp and the next day there was a door but no handle."

"We're going to install a locking mechanism on this side as

well," Linda explained. "You guys can figure out how you'll schedule opening the doors. My daughter volunteered to paint a mural on the cafe side, if that's all right."

Zoe stared at Elba with big eyes.

She shrugged. "That's fine with me. Let me know when she needs access."

"Great. I'll get you her number and you can work that out with her directly."

A customer peeked through the opening. "Oh wow. Is this going to be a bookstore?"

"Yes," Zoe said.

"That's so cool. When do you open?" the woman asked.

"Eight weeks, give or take."

"I can't wait. It'll be great not to have to go to Fayetteville or Raleigh to go to the bookstore." She left with a wave to Elba.

"I'm so excited!" Elba bounced on her toes and clapped her hands. "I need to get back to the counter. One of my waitresses called in sick and my other one can't get a babysitter on such short notice. Stop by before you leave?"

"Of course."

"Let me show you the rest of the work we've done and what we have left," Linda said.

They left the cafe and Linda closed the bookcase behind them, showing Zoe exactly how the latches worked and how to ensure they were closed.

An hour later, she was no less nervous about the decision she'd made, but her excitement was on the same level and on track to surpass her worries. She could do this. No. She was doing it.

Exiting out the front, she walked around to the cafe and entered the normal way. When she got to the counter, Elba was talking on her cell, visibly upset. She hung up and clenched her phone in her fist.

"I hate him. I hate him. I hate him so fucking much."

"Dipshit?" Zoe asked.

"Yes. It's his week. The deal is supposed to be that when it's his week, he deals with everything unless it's life or death. When it's my week, I deal with it. April doesn't feel well and went to the school nurse who said she's running a low-grade fever and should go home. Except ass-clown is busy and I need to do it. Know what he's busy with? Paperwork so he can make his pickup basketball game. Because his stupid, out-of-shape, white-guys-can't-jump basketball game is more important than his daughter. It's not like I have a business to run or anything or that I'm short staffed. No, that doesn't matter to him at all. I wish he would keel over and die and I'm such a horrible person for wishing that."

Zoe walked around the counter and hugged her. Elba sagged in her arms.

"Stop. Take a deep breath. How about if I go pick her up?"

Elba lifted her head. "You can't. You're not on the list. Although I was going to ask if I can add you in case anything like this happened again."

"Of course. You can't call the school and let them know I'm picking her up?"

She shook her head. "I wish. I've tried to do that before. They're adamant that it has to be someone that is prearranged with the school in writing. Too many divorced couples getting their new significant other to pick the kid up and the ex losing their shit at the school for allowing it."

"Ah. Yeah. I can see how that might cause issues." She cocked her head. "I can stay here while you go get her."

"Really? You'd do that?"

"As long as I don't have to cook."

Elba's laugh was full of relief. "No. Rob does all the cooking. I'll introduce you. He's good. A student at the local culinary school. All you have to do is take the orders and keep the coffee fresh. Maybe heat up some pie."

"I can heat up some pie," Zoe said.

Elba hugged her. "Thank you. Let me show you how to work

the register. I'll bring April back here and she can rest on the couch in my office with a cup of tea."

She walked Zoe through the register, which was really a touch screen attached to a money till, not an actual register, and was thankfully user-friendly. The espresso machine was a little more confusing, but was computerized and not one of the fancy manual espresso machines.

"I don't have time for that," was Elba's response when she asked.

ALMOST FIVE HOURS LATER, Zoe pulled into her driveway, shut off her car, and rested her head against the steering wheel. How could she have forgotten how exhausting waitressing was? It wasn't that it had been difficult, although she'd gotten a couple of orders mixed up, it was being on her feet and constantly on the go. How the hell did Elba do that six and a half days a week? By herself with only another waitress?

Zoe had sucked it up because she owed her big time for all the additional help she'd given her by taking care of the in-person issues with the bookstore.

The takeout box Rob had given her after they'd shut down and cleaned up smelled delicious and her stomach rumbled. Right. Dinner, shower, bed. Climbing out of her car, her gaze was drawn to Tim's house almost against her will. Who was she kidding? She'd seen his truck in the drive when she'd pulled up and wondered if he'd stop by again like he had the other night. More than once she'd wondered if he'd only stopped by because Mrs. Wilson had said something about the moving truck or because he wanted to see her again. Did she want to see him again?

The tiny flutter in her stomach said yes. Her mind might tell her she didn't have time for a guy right now and she needed to stay focused on her bookstore, but she missed the companionship of having someone in her life. Friends were great, but she wanted someone to cuddle with on the couch at the end of a long day.

A woman walked out of his front door, then turned back around to face the house.

Zoe ducked down behind her car. Wait? What was she doing? There was no reason to hide—she was the neighbor.

"*Tolo.*" She stood up and checked out the woman.

Tall, with dark blond hair and a strong physique, she was the physical antithesis of Zoe. The woman waved toward the front door and walked to the older SUV parked on the road in front of Tim's house.

She might not be a supermodel, but she was still beautiful. "Of course she is," Zoe muttered. She might want a cuddle buddy, but it looked like Tim already had one.

CHAPTER 7

Z oe wandered into the antique furniture stall at the weekend market, sipping her iced coffee.

"What are we looking for exactly?" her sister asked.

"I'll know it when I see it."

"That's very helpful," Gabby said. "I'm going to go look at t-shirts."

Zoe gazed heavenward and again wondered what made her tell her sister her plans for the day. She'd mentioned shopping and weekend market and her sister had not only invited herself along, but drove over two hours to do it. She'd wanted to "see for herself" that Zoe was okay.

She loved her family but as the youngest, they had a tendency to baby her. Especially now, after the divorce.

She'd had a successful career in the Air Force and was starting her own business. She'd been to war, for crying out loud. Well, not really. She'd been to Iraq and Afghanistan and even though she hadn't been shooting at bad guys, it had sucked and completely changed her whole outlook on life.

But none of that mattered to her family. They viewed her decision to separate from the military and follow her passion to be nothing more than a whim. A lot of people would argue getting out of the service after ten or more years was wasted effort, but she didn't see it that way. Getting out was the opportunity to do what she wanted for herself. Not because the Air Force told her she had to or because she was following along after someone else's career aspirations.

The bookstore was for her. She didn't have the words to explain why it was so important, she just needed her family to be supportive.

She squeezed between a large frame and a standing lamp. She didn't expect to find anything, but she'd thought that before. Her knowledge of antiques was a big, shallow pool of *nada*. She couldn't look at something and know when it was made or how much it was worth. It could be two years old or two hundred years old. What she saw was the story. She imagined the people who used it; the kids who scratched their names into the top of an old school desk; the family who sat around a dining room table; the woman who set her bookmarked novel on the small bedside table. When she looked at a battered piece of furniture, she didn't see the dings or neglect, she saw the finished product—and its new story.

It was the same with her bookstore. She could see it in her mind's eye. Muted colors and soft lighting. Comfortable chairs that invited people to sit and read. Dark cherry bookcases filled with books waiting to be picked next. She'd been enthralled with the idea of a private library ever since she'd seen the movie *Dangerous Beauty,* and while she didn't need to turn to prostitution to have access to books, there were times the idea seemed as outrageous and she second-guessed herself. Then she looked at her business plan and went over her checklists and everything righted itself.

Her goal was in sight. All she needed to do was follow the path she'd laid out to reach it.

A small, yellow table caught her eye. Moving the basket of

tchotchkes from the top, she knelt down next to it. The edges were chipped, revealing several layers of paint. It needed to be stripped and refinished, but it was well-made and would fit nicely between the two leather seats she'd found last month before she'd left Arizona.

"Can I help you find something?"

Zoe stood and found an older woman next to her.

"How much do you want for the table?"

"It's a nice piece of furniture," the woman said.

Hmm... She was either getting ready to try to swindle Zoe or she was hoping for a good haggle. Either way, she had no idea what she was getting into. Zoe's mother had once made a carpet vendor in Izmir cry and she was her mother's daughter.

RIDING a euphoric high from getting a good price for the table, she found Gabby in a stall full of tourist trinkets and t-shirts.

"Can't you find these in Charlotte?" she asked.

"These say Haven Springs on them. The only ones I can find in Charlotte say Charlotte on them."

Zoe's stomach rumbled. They'd been wandering the outdoor flea market for a while and she was hungry.

"Are you ready to eat? I told Elba we'd have lunch at the cafe."

"Shoot! What time is it? I told Alex I'd be home around five." Forgetting she was holding her almost empty frappuccino cup, Gabby tilted her hand to look at her watch.

"Don't—!"

"Ahh!"

She righted the cup, dribbling a light brown stream of liquid across a half a dozen or more stacks of t-shirts.

Zoe stared, her mouth agape.

"Meu Deus. O que devo fazer?"

"Find—"

Gabby shoved the cup at Zoe and rushed out of the stall, not bothering to look back.

Zoe stared at her retreating back. "Are you serious?"

She was going to kill Gabby. She didn't need to worry about getting home to her husband and three boys because her body was going to be buried in a shallow grave somewhere along the highway.

A throat cleared behind her. "Is she coming back?" The deep timbre sent shivers down her spine.

She'd only heard it a few times, but she recognized Tim's voice. His was the only one that had ever caused that kind of reaction. Pressing her lips together, she turned slowly to face him. Or his chest since she barely reached his shoulders. It was a nice chest too, snuggly wrapped in a gray Carolina Panthers t-shirt. She tilted her head up and took a step back to be able to see more of him.

Her lady bits swooned and she had a sudden urge to fan herself and say things like "fiddle-dee-dee."

Maybe it was being back in the south, but there was something about a guy in a beat-up ball cap that did it for her. It framed his face, accentuating the squareness of his jaw. His eyes were shadowed under the bill, but she remembered their color and how bright they'd seemed surrounded by dark lashes.

"Well?"

"What?"

He pointed in the direction her sister had run. "Is she coming back to pay for all this?"

She glanced over her shoulder, remembering the coffee that had been drizzled over the shirts. Her shoulders sagged.

"Highly unlikely. If I know Gabby, she's waiting around the corner to say how sorry she is I got caught."

"Gabby, your sister?"

She tried not to stare as he slipped his hands into the front pockets of his well-worn jeans.

"Unfortunately."

"Oh my God! My mom is going to kill me!" A teenager rushed over to them and frantically picked up the stained merchandise. "What am I going to do?"

Zoe rested a hand on the girl's arm. "I'm so sorry. I didn't realize I had anything left in my cup and I tipped it over. I'll pay for all the shirts."

"Really?" the girl asked with tears in her eyes.

"Of course. It's my fault. And I know how mothers can be, believe me."

"Thank you. She'd seriously ground me until I graduate if I told her all these shirts were ruined."

They gathered up the shirts and Zoe followed her to the corner where the register sat.

"Do you like working in the market?" she asked.

"Not really. It's hot during the summer and there isn't a lot of traffic in the off-season, but I have time to study between customers."

"What are you studying?"

"AP chemistry right now." She bagged the shirts and lowered her gaze. "There's eleven shirts. You can get six for the price of five, so if you get one more..." She shrugged her shoulder.

Zoe smiled. "What's your name?"

"Beth."

"I'll grab another shirt."

Tim waited near the scene of the crime. "You're covering for your sister."

"What else am I supposed to do?"

"Call your sister and tell her to come back and pay for them?"

"Oh, she'll pay me back." She picked up a bright pink tank top with "Carolina Girl" in white letters. "I know all her secrets."

She finished paying and walked over to where Tim waited, leaning against the side of a building. "Want a souvenir shirt?"

He grinned at her. "Got any that say 'southern boys do it better'?"

Nossa Senhora. He had a dimple. Not a cute little girl dimple, more like a Tom Selleck dimple that divided his left cheek.

Her entire lower body clenched. *Did* they do it better? *Stop! He has a girlfriend. A tall, gorgeous girlfriend.*

He didn't wait for her answer...or provide one of his own. "Going to get your sister?"

"Yes. We're supposed to go to my friend's cafe for lunch. Gabby's paying."

Damn it, he smiled again.

"I'm heading that way." He tilted his head the same direction she was headed.

"That's the way I'm going as well."

He held out an arm, indicating she should lead the way.

"Did you get, uh...unpacked?" He cleared his throat.

"The boxes are unpacked. I still need to put some stuff away."

"Hmm." He stepped behind her as they passed a family pushing a stroller, using his hand on her lower back to steer her through the crowd.

The gentle pressure of his fingers at the base of her spine sent tingles racing up to the fine hairs at the base of her neck and she barely repressed the shiver they caused.

CHAPTER 8

Tim took the opportunity of the narrow sidewalk and large family to place his hand on Zoe's lower back. A small shiver raced down her back and goosebumps rose on the back of her neck. From his touch? Could she be as affected by him as he was by her? It had taken all his willpower not to pull on the thick curl that had escaped the pile of hair on top of her head and he'd only managed by shoving his hands in the pockets of his jeans.

She'd been really nice to the girl manning the booth and he didn't think it had anything to do with him standing there. He hadn't given her a lot of time to react between when her sister dribbled coffee on the t-shirts and when he'd approached, but he had a feeling she would have done the right thing regardless.

"Does your sister always leave you holding the bag? Or the cup, in this case?"

"I've taken the blame for her on more than occasion. I always got off light because I'm the baby of the family."

"Huh."

She turned caramel colored eyes up to him. "What 'huh?'"

"I have a younger sister. She's the baby. Now that I think of it, she got away with a lot more than my brother and I did."

"Did you blame her for things you did?"

He chuckled. "There was no way my parents would have believed Shannon did the things we did."

She flashed him a smile. It felt like a punch in the gut. He had a suspicion he would do just about anything to make her smile like that again.

"Gabriella." A hard tone entered her voice.

The sisters were of similar height and build, but Gabriella's face was fuller and her hair wasn't as curly.

"*Desculpa, caro.*"

Zoe removed the clean pink shirt and held the bag out to Gabriella. "You owe me fifty dollars."

Her sister responded in Portuguese. His gaze jumped between the two women as they argued. His two-years of high school Spanish in no way equipped him to keep up with, much less understand, their conversation.

"Gabriella?" he asked.

The sisters stopped arguing and Gabriella finally took notice of him. She looked him up and down, then pointed at him. "*Quem e?*"

Zoe sighed. "Tim, this is my sister Gabriella. Gabby, this is Tim. The neighbor."

Gabby held out a hand. "It's a pleasure to meet you, Neighbor Tim."

The way she rolled her *r* made it sound like she purred when she spoke. Hell, she might have.

"You too," he said.

Gabby spoke to Zoe in Portuguese while she continued to look at him.

Fifteen years on the police force had taught him there were usually only a few of reasons for people to not speak English—they didn't know it, weren't comfortable speaking it, or they were talking about a person but didn't want that person to know what they were saying.

Both Zoe and her sister spoke English with almost no trace of an accent, so... "Are you talking about me?"

Zoe blushed and Gabby smirked.

"I was saying—"

"How very sorry she was for being such a horrible and irresponsible sister and of course she will not only pay me back, but buy me lunch as well," Zoe said.

"That's not—"

"Isn't that right, Gabriella?" Zoe spoke through clenched teeth and glared at his sister.

She glared back before batting her eyes at Tim. "Zoe was explaining that you saw the accident with the t-shirts. I panicked. I would have returned and paid for the shirts, but I saw Zoe had already taken care of it."

Not knowing either sister well enough to know if that was true, he nodded.

"We should go," Zoe said. "I said we'd be there at twelve-thirty."

"We're meeting a friend for lunch," Gabby said. "Would you like to join us?"

"I'd love to, but I'm meeting my brother and his fiancée."

"That's too bad," Gabby said.

"Some other time." He looked at Zoe. "I'm sure we'll run into each other again, being neighbors and all."

Zoe licked her lips, causing more than a few erotic thoughts to flood his brain. He adjusted his ball cap, then shoved his hands in his pockets. Jase and Bree were probably waiting for him but he wanted to linger, to spend even a few more minutes next to Zoe, but it was starting to get awkward.

"See you around."

"Bye," they both said.

The switched back to Portuguese as he walked away and he grinned, fighting the urge to look back over his shoulder. They were definitely talking about him. Maybe they were checking out his butt.

∽

A SMALL BELL over the door jangled as he pushed into the small restaurant Bree said she wanted to try. Dozens of different kinds of pastries filled the display case to his left, calling out to his sweet tooth, *eat me*. Whatever kind of food they served here, he was saving room for dessert. Hell, he might have only dessert. And one to go.

A young girl walked around the counter, holding a long menu folder. "Welcome to the Cafe. Will you be dining alone or will others be joining you this afternoon?"

Tim stared down at her. She was very articulate for someone so young. He took in her long blond hair, gathered in a braid that hung over her shoulder and her bright blue eyes.

"How old are you?"

Her weary sigh and barely contained eye roll told him it wasn't the first time she'd been asked that question.

"I'm thirteen. I only work six hours a week. My mom owns the Cafe and I'm trying to earn tips to help pay for a school trip to New York."

She'd definitely recited that more than a few times. Over her head, he spotted Jase exiting a short hall at the back of the dining area.

Tim pointed in that direction. "The rest of my party is already here."

She turned to follow his gestured and then flashed a smile. "Perfect. I was getting their waters ready. I'll be right over to take drink orders."

Spinning so quickly he had to dodge the whip-like action of her braid, she headed back behind the counter next to the pastry display. He wove through the dozen or so tables occupied with couples and small groups in various stages of their meals to the back of the restaurant and the long table against the back wall.

Planting a kiss on Bree's cheek, he thumped Jase on the back of his head and took the empty seat across from them, next to Denise.

"Hey. Where's Chris?" He hardly ever saw Denise without her husband attached to her. Thursday had been the first time in weeks he'd seen her alone.

"Went to see a man about a boat," Denise said.

He glanced behind her chair at the large, canine-shaped mound that was her service dog, Sprocket. Straightening up, he asked, "Is that because you already have a horse?"

"Ha, ha, ha, ha," she fake laughed.

He grinned. There'd been a time when he'd thought about asking Denise out, but after spending some time with her he knew they'd never have worked out. She was too independent. Not that he had anything against independent women, but he needed at least the illusion of being needed. It wasn't ego. He enjoyed taking care of a woman. He wasn't going to apologize for being an old-fashioned romantic—even if that didn't get him a lot of dates nowadays.

"How's the old lady doing?" Denise asked.

"You were right. She's in the running for the laziest dog in the world. If I didn't walk her, I'm not even sure she would move to go to the bathroom."

"Told you," she said with a smirk.

"I'm still not adopting her."

The girl approached their table with a tray loaded down with glasses of water and a basket of bread.

He popped up and helped her set the glasses on the table while she placed the basket of bread in the middle.

"Thank you," she said.

"Can I get a straw?" Jase asked.

She flipped her tray over and held it in front of her. "There are reusable straws with your silverware."

Bree picked up her napkin-wrapped utensils and pulled out a long, silver tube. "It's metal."

"Stainless steel. Americans use five-hundred million plastic straw each day, most of which end up in landfills or the ocean where they kill thousands of birds and sea life each year."

Bree looked at her straw. "That's so sad." She slapped Jase on the chest with the back of her hand, making him flinch. "We're getting reusable straws."

"Okay," he grunted.

Tim's lips twitched. He'd give Jase shit about being whipped, but it looked good on him.

"Have you had a chance to look over the menus?" the girl asked.

He hadn't. He opened the menu in front of him. "Is there a dessert only option?"

"We do have the dessert lunch," she said.

His head snapped up. "The what?"

She leaned over and pointed.

The Save Room Special.

"It's the quiche of the day and your choice of a half salad and pastry. The warm goat cheese and fig salad with balsamic vinaigrette is my favorite. It comes with walnuts so if you decide that's what you want, let me know if you have any allergies."

"I'm sold," Denise said.

"Me too. No allergies." Bree said. "Are we waiting for Chris?"

"No. I'm starving. He can order when he gets here." Denise held her menu out to the girl.

Tim made a show of glancing over the menu, but he was sold as well. "I'll have the same."

"What? No steamed chicken and grilled vegetables?" Jase asked.

"Shut up." It was steamed vegetables and grilled chicken and it was easy. Bland, but easy, which was one of the reasons the delicious smell of fresh bread was causing his mouth to salivate.

"I'll have the French dip," Jase said.

"You're a dip," Tim said. Not very mature, but when were brothers ever?

Jase grinned. "And can I get extra meat, please?"

"Of course. Did anyone want anything other than water to drink?"

Everyone replied with a negative.

"Great, I'll put those orders in right away."

She took Jase and Tim's menus and left the table. Seconds later a high-pitched shriek rent the air.

Sprocket let out a deep woof.

Tim shoved back his chair as he stood and pivoted, reaching for his service revolver. Which he didn't have. So stupid. He should have sat facing the door, then he could have seen the threat of...

Zoe and her sister?

CHAPTER 9

A much younger version of Elba screamed and catapulted herself into Zoe's arms.

"Aunt Zoe! Oh my god! You're here! You're here!" She jumped up and down, jarring Zoe's chin with her shoulder, causing her teeth to snap together.

The doors of the kitchen flew open and Elba burst through. "April, what on earth?"

Zoe watched the worry melt to a smile.

"Hey, you made it."

"I take it you didn't tell her I was coming and that she's feeling better?"

"Yeah." She turned to the dining room. "Sorry, everyone—family reunion."

Their audience returned to their lunches. Except for the tall man standing in the back corner...next to the beautiful woman she'd seen leaving his house two days ago.

The universe was a bully. What had she ever done to deserve such bad luck?

April bounced on her toes, still excited by Zoe's surprise appearance.

"*Calma*. I'm happy to see you too, *caro*."

"April, don't you have orders to put in?" Elba took her by the shoulders and pulled her away from Zoe.

"Mom," she whined.

"No 'mom.' You wanted to work. This is part of working."

"Ugh." April's shoulders drooped and she dragged her feet but trudged to the computer behind the counter.

"Sorry. I've been slammed. Sabrina, my waitress that was sick? Morning sickness, but the kind that lasts all day. You know a man came up with that phrase, right? Morning sickness, my ass."

"Mmm. I was nauseous twenty-four hours a day for sixteen weeks with all three of my boys. I finally told my husband if he didn't get the doctor to snip him, I was going to do it myself."

Zoe sighed. At least Gabby came by her nickname naturally. "Elba, my sister Gabby. Gabby, Elba."

"It's so nice to finally meet you!" Gabby pulled Elba into a hug and then kissed her on both cheeks.

"Oh! We're kissing," Elba said.

"*Claro*. In Brazil, we kiss."

"I don't remember you ever kissing anyone like that," Elba said to Zoe.

"That's because the first time I tried to do that a girl called me a spic dyke, so I never did it again."

Gabby and Elba both gaped.

"You never told us that," Gabby said

"Oh my god. How old were you?" Elba asked.

"I was twelve, probably." She looked at Gabby. "We had just moved to the States. I didn't want to cause any trouble."

Gabby clucked her tongue. "You should have told us."

"It was a long time ago. Can we eat? I'm starving."

April skipped up next to them. "Is the reserved table for them? It's back here."

She led the way to their table without waiting for an answer. It was right next to Tim and his friends. Of course it was.

Elba stopped short. "Oh, hey. Your stripper-gram is here. I didn't even see him come in. Tim, right?"

"What's a stripper-gram?" April asked, timing her questioned perfectly with their arrival at the table.

"Tim is a stripper-gram? I thought he was a police officer," Gabby said.

If she looked in the mirror right now, her hair would be flaming red. It would have to be, judging by the intense heat trying to burst from her skin. She'd never blushed so hard in her life, not even when she'd been teased in school.

"Stripper-gram? You moonlighting, big brother?"

Even if he hadn't addressed Tim as brother, the resemblance pegged them as family. Whereas Tim's hair was lighter and he was more clean cut and lean muscle, his brother was bulkier and wilder around the edges.

"Zoe, this...person is my brother, Jase. His fiancée, Bree—I have yet to figure out what she sees in my brother—and this is Denise."

He didn't put a label on Denise. Because she didn't have one or because she didn't need one?

"Everyone, this is my new neighbor, Zoe, and her sister, Gabby. I stopped by after work one day to see how Zoe was settling in. I was still in my uniform and some assumptions were made."

The fiancée, Bree, leaned an elbow on the table and rested her chin on the palm of her hand. "Oh, yeah. I can totally see that."

His brother covered her eyes. "Quit seeing it. Now."

Bree moved his hand from her face and held it to her chest as she whispered something to him. He pulled back and looked at Tim.

"Bree wants to know if I can borrow one of your uniforms."

She hit him on the arm. "Don't ask him that!"

"You just told me to."

"Not *here*!"

"The answer's no," Tim said. "Even if you soaked it lye and bleach before you had it dry cleaned, I would still have to burn it and those things are expensive."

Zoe didn't understand the dynamic that was happening. Her family had never joked around like that—even when they were kids. They'd fought and argued, but hardly ever teased in such a fun and light-hearted manner. Her ex had never been that way either. Not with her anyway.

"Well, we'll let you get back to your lunch," she said.

"You should join us," Bree said.

"Oh, no. We wouldn't want to intrude."

"You're not intruding," Denise said. "We'll pull the other table over and there'll be plenty of room."

Of course she would be nice. Tim was nice. Why wouldn't his girlfriend be nice as well? Would it be too much to ask that she have a flaw? Bitchy was a flaw.

Mentally slapping her forehead, Zoe told herself to snap out of it. She wasn't looking for romance and especially not with someone who was taken.

Tables and chairs scraped across the poured concrete floor and before she could voice another objection, she was seated across from Tim and Denise.

Perfeito.

"BABY JESUS HATES ME," she mumbled in Portuguese.

Gabby picked up her water glass. "Don't let mama hear you blaspheme and baby Jesus doesn't hate you."

"Pretty sure he does."

"Well, if he does it's because you make him cry."

Denise choked on her water and pressed her hand to her mouth.

"*Tu fala português?*" Zoe asked. What were the odds of that?

She shook her head and cleared her throat. "No, but I can understand Spanish pretty well. Not a great speaker though."

"Where did you learn Spanish?" Gabby asked.

"My dad was stationed in El Paso, Texas when I was younger—before we moved to North Carolina. I picked up more when I was in the Army."

"Zoe was in the Air Force," Gabby said.

Bree leaned around Jase and held up her hand. "Go Air Force!"

Jase leaned back as Zoe leaned around his other side and slapped her palm against Bree's. "What did you do?"

"I was a med tech, then I was on a Cultural Support Team."

"Oh, wow. Really?" That was pretty badass. She'd met a few on her last deployment. That was not an easy job.

"Yeah. What about you?"

"Contracting. Not nearly as exciting as CST, though."

"When did you get out?" Denise asked.

Zoe turned her attention across the table and felt the full force of Tim's gaze. "I'm still on terminal."

"Nice. Where are you coming from?"

"What's terminal?" Tim asked.

"Luke Air Force Base in Arizona." She looked at Tim. "Terminal leave. I'm technically still on active duty, but I had almost seventy days of leave saved up, so I'm burning that until my actual separation date."

"How long were you in?" he asked.

Gabby leaned forward. "More than thirteen years. She only had seven more years until she could retire." She switched back to Portuguese and looked at Zoe. "A waste."

"Can we not go through this again? Please?" she pleaded in English.

"When it's time, it's time," Denise said with a shrug. "Sometimes you don't have any more to give."

Zoe's shoulder's sagged. She really didn't want to like Denise, but it was hard not to like someone who immediately came to her defense.

"Did you guys grow up in Brazil or the U.S.?" Tim asked.

Whether he asked out of genuine curiosity or as a way to change the subject, she didn't care. She could kiss him for it—in a completely platonic way of course. Her gaze unwillingly dropped to his lips. Not the thoughts she should be having.

Before she could answer, a well-built, tattooed guy with a buzz cut stopped at their table and poked Tim in the shoulder. "Dude. You're in my seat."

Tim stared up at him. "Am I? I didn't see your name on it."

"I can make you move."

Holy cow. They were going to fight. Right here in Elba's restaurant.

CHAPTER 10

Denise smacked Tim on the upper arm with the back of her hand.

"Ow." He grabbed his bicep as if it had it hurt.

"Quit antagonizing him," she said.

"But it's fun." He pushed the chair back and stood, slapping Chris on the shoulder. "Nice of you to show up."

He took a chair from a neighboring table and sat at the end of theirs, putting Zoe on his left. Too bad Chris had shown up—Tim'd had a great view of Zoe. If he could only figure out why she'd avoided looking at him. Was she still embarrassed that he'd witnessed her sister spilling coffee on those shirts?

She looked between him and Chris with a look of confusion.

"Zoe, this is my husband, Chris," Denise said.

"Husband? I thought..." She glanced from Denise to him, a faint blush staining her cheeks.

"Oh, God no!" Denise said.

Tim clutched his chest. "Oh! Straight to the heart."

"Whatever."

He could actually hear Denise roll her eyes.

The young girl, who he'd figured out was April from their

earlier conversation appeared with another menu, followed by Elba.

"I know most of you have ordered. I was going to use Zoe and Gabby as guinea pigs for some new menu items. Would y'all be interested or would you prefer to stick with what you ordered?"

Everyone glanced around the table at each other.

"I'm game," Bree said.

Denise shrugged. "Sure."

"One question," Tim said.

Elba raised her eyebrows. "Shoot."

"Does it include dessert?"

"It'd better," Zoe said. "That's the only reason I agreed to this."

Elba poked her in the shoulder. "Shut up. You love my food. I'll put some platters together." She looked at April. "Can you get them plates and then go check on the other tables?"

"On it."

Tim watched mother and daughter retreat, then shifted his attention back to Zoe. "So back to my question before we were so rudely interrupted—did you grow up in Brazil or the U.S.?"

Gabby set her water glass on the table. "Both. Our birth father passed away when Zoe was five. Our mom worked at the American Consulate in São Paulo and met our step-father a few years later when he was assigned there. He adopted us after they married."

"You didn't take your step-father's last name when he adopted you?" He hadn't felt comfortable asking the one and only time he'd met Brian and Marianna in person.

"Our mother wanted us to keep a part of our father," Zoe explained. "Brian, our step-father, understood."

"I'm so sorry to hear about your father," Bree said. "I know how hard it is to lose a parent."

Jase kissed her temple.

"Thank you," Zoe said. "I think it was harder for Gabby and our older brother. I only have vague memories of our father."

Trying to change the subject from the depressing turn it had taken, Tim asked, "Are you going to be working at the base?"

"No, I'm opening my own business," Zoe said.

Gabby said something in Portuguese. Zoe closed her eyes and took a deep breath, blowing it out through pursed lips. This must be a contentious topic between the sisters.

"What kind of business?" he asked.

"A bookstore."

Bree set her glass down with a thud and leaned around Jase. "Did you say a bookstore?"

"Yes?"

Pushing her chair back, Bree stood and tapped Jase's shoulder. "Switch seats with me."

Shooting Bree an amused look, he obliged and took her seat against the wall, switching their water glasses as he sat.

Denise pushed back her chair, dislodging Sprocket behind her. Walking around Chris and Gabby, she waved her hand at Tim. "You too."

"But I like my seat," he said. "And I've already had to move once."

"Timothy," she said with a warning in her voice.

"Fine." It was anything but fine. He wanted to stay in his seat next to Zoe where he occasionally caught a whiff of her soft floral scent. Chris probably smelled like...

"Why do you smell like motor oil and fish?"

"I was checking out a boat." He glanced at Bree and Denise, crowded around Zoe. "This is how I lose my wife. She's going to leave me to go live in a bookstore now that she knows someone who owns one."

Elba and April returned, and Elba explained what each dish was as she set the large platters down in the center of the table. "Does anyone need anything else?"

"I'm good. This looks so delicious." Bree looked up from the spread. "Thank you."

Elba grinned. "Let me know how you like everything."

"Does she cater?" Bree asked after Elba had moved to another table. "Because if the food tastes as good as it looks, I might need her to do the food for our reception."

"I don't know," Zoe said. "I know she wants to expand into dinner service, so she may."

"I thought you were grilling," Tim said.

Jase's eyes bugged out and he mouthed, *you are dead.* Bree sat up straight and slowly turned her head to look at Jase.

"Oh boy," Denise murmured.

"Country wedding does not translate to redneck backyard barbecue." Bree's voice rose at the end.

"Babe, it was just a suggestion to help save money."

Bree pointed her fork at him. "Don't 'babe' me. We're already saving money by having it at the house. And Gran is paying for the reception."

"You know how I feel about that," he said.

"Feel free to discuss your misgivings with her." Bree picked up a mini quiche and ate it while staring him down. She stopped glaring at him to look down at her plate. "Oh my god. This is so good. I really hope she caters."

She closed her eyes and moaned as she chewed. Jase leaned closer, whispered in her ear. She glared at him for a moment, then kissed him. "I'm still annoyed."

Zoe cleared her throat. A deep blush covered her cheeks—she must have overheard whatever Jase had said to Bree.

"Denise, if you're looking for new book recommendations, you should follow Mr. Romance's blog."

Tim frowned. "Is it really a guy?"

Zoe's gold-flecked gaze met his. "Yes, he's a librarian in New York."

"Huh."

"Why do you say it like that?" Her voice carried an edge of annoyance.

"I don't know any guys that would admit to reading romance."

"Maybe you need to meet better guys." She took a sip of water while staring at him.

He made a note to himself not to make any disparaging remarks about romance books.

"I've read a couple of romance novels," Chris said.

"Really?" Gabby asked.

"After I woke up to Denise bawling her eyes out one night, damn straight."

"Seriously?" Denise asked. "You couldn't have said you read them out of curiosity?"

"I was curious why you were crying about a book. Getting some pointers from the sex scenes didn't hurt." He took a bite of food and smirked as he chewed.

"Are you always like this?" Gabby asked.

"Like what?" Bree asked.

"Pretty much," Tim said at the same time.

Someone's phone pinged and everyone glanced at their screens. Gabby swore under her breath and shoved her phone back into her purse. "I'm sorry, I need to go. My adult husband is apparently incapable of handling the duties of parenthood by himself."

She stood and eased out from between Chris and Tim. Swinging her purse over her shoulder, she walked around the table to Zoe and kissed her on the cheek. They had a short conversation in Portuguese that made Denise choke into her hand and Gabby left.

Zoe pursed her lips and looked under the table. "Tim, can you hand me the bag of t-shirts she left under her seat?"

Sure enough, Gabby had left the bag of shirts on the floor. He handed her the bag. "Did she pay you for them?"

"Of course not."

"Did she do that on purpose?"

"There's no telling with Gabby. She was always the one

causing the trouble but never getting into trouble when we were growing up."

Tim looked at Jase. "Sounds like someone else I know."

Jase pointed his fork at him. "I got my butt spanked plenty, big bro. Don't even try it."

"I should probably be going as well," Zoe said. "I still have some boxes to unpack and I want to have the house ready before I have to start on the store."

"I still can't believe I know someone who's opening a bookstore," Bree said. "I'm so excited!"

"Let us know if you need any help, especially if you need recommendations for books to order," Denise added.

Zoe laughed. "I will. Thank you for the offer. I'm going to say goodbye to Elba. It was very nice meeting you all."

"Wait!" Bree picked up her phone from the table. "Let me get your number."

"Me too," Denise said.

They exchanged numbers and Zoe left after talking to Elba and hugging April. All of a sudden, the afternoon seemed less exciting. Less bright. As if an overhead light had been turned off, dimming the room slightly.

His phone pinged. Hoping for a call for work that would give him an excuse to follow after Zoe and catch up, he looked at the screen. Denise had shared Zoe's phone number.

"What did you do that for?"

"Just helping out."

THE DOG LIFTED HER HEAD, looked at the back door, and barked once. Laying her head back on the dog bed, she shifted her eyes and stared at Tim as if to say, "Are you going to take care of that?"

Her excess movement was unusual enough to pique Tim's

interest. He pushed up from the couch and opened the sliding door to the backyard.

"Are you coming?" he asked the dog.

She groaned and sighed at the same time, a good indication that she was not going to go out with him. She'd done her part to alert him to whatever was out there, the rest was up to him.

"Bree was not kidding. You are the laziest dog that ever lazed." Shaking his head, he stepped out on the small deck and scanned the yard.

His house backed up to a copse that hid the houses behind his and provided a semblance of privacy. One of the upsides of buying a house in a more established neighborhood, which was realtor speak for 'old'.

"What do you want?"

He glanced sharply to his left and saw Zoe standing in almost the exact spot in her backyard that he stood in his. She was staring at something in the yard just beyond the weak pool of light cast by the bulb near the door. She really needed a couple of floodlights for the backyard.

"I don't care. I got stuck in a window because of you. Do you know how embarrassing that was?"

"Who are you talking to?" he asked.

She shrieked and something ran into the trees.

"*Puta merda!*" She leaned forward with a hand over her chest. "You scared the shit out of me. Why are you lurking in the dark?"

"I'm not lurking. I'm standing outside my house." He crossed the yard so he could talk to her without yelling. "What were you doing?"

She stared into the darkness behind the house. "Yelling at the raccoon."

"The key-thieving raccoon?"

"Yes."

"How do you know it was the same one?"

She shrugged. "I don't, I just assumed it was the same one and it had come back to taunt me. Or beg for food. Maybe both."

"If you feed it, it'll keep coming back," he said.

"I know, which is why didn't give it any food."

Tim held his hands up. "I'm just saying. They look cute, but they are a nuisance."

"Yes, I got stuck in a window because of one."

He grinned and crossed his arms, wishing he could see more of her legs, but Zoe was wearing loose pajama pants. "You're blaming your bad decisions on a raccoon?"

"It's was the raccoon's fault. If it hadn't stolen my keys, I wouldn't have been locked out, and been forced to try to climb in a window." She braced her hands on her hips. "In fact, I think Lifetime should do a special on the dangers of being led astray by devious raccoons."

He had no idea what she was talking about. The t-shirt she wore pulled against her breasts, highlighting the fact that she wasn't wearing a bra. He quickly came to the conclusion that he was a very weak man. The outline of her breasts under the thin material was going to be seared in his mind all night long.

"What?"

"Nothing. Never mind. I'm going to..." She pointed at the sliding door. "Go inside. Good night."

Before he could form a thought or ask her to dinner, she disappeared into the house and he heard the lock click.

"'Night." He was talking to a closed door. *Smooth. Real smooth.*

CHAPTER 11

Tim turned out of the parking lot of the retirement home where he and Kevin had finished a courtesy call.

"How often do you do this?" Kevin asked.

"I try to stop by at least a couple times a month."

"Why?"

He glanced at his young partner. "My grandfather had to go into a home after my grandmother passed away. He had mobility issues and wasn't able to take care of himself. It was really depressing seeing all the other people who didn't have anyone visiting them, so I started spending as much time with other residents as I could. I kept doing it after he died."

"That's really cool. Both sets of grandparents passed away when I was young, so I never knew them very well."

Kevin's cell phone rang. Glancing at it, he sighed but answered. "Officer Moore...I told you I wasn't able to today...Call 9-1-1 and let them know you think he's there...I don't know if we'll answer the call...All right, I'll see what I can do."

He hung up and looked at Tim. "Do you remember that girl from the domestic disturbance a few weeks ago? The one I gave my card to?"

The hairs on the back of Tim's neck stood up. "Yes."

"She's been calling non-stop. I haven't encouraged her and I keep trying to put her off, but she won't stop calling. Somehow she found out what gym I go to and she got a membership there. I've even seen her a few times in the grocery store. She swears it's coincidence, but it's too random."

"Okay…" Tim wasn't sure where Kevin was going with the conversation.

"That was her. She said she thinks her ex is outside her apartment and she doesn't feel safe."

"What do you think?" He glanced at Kevin who shrugged and shook his head.

"I don't know. I told her if she really felt unsafe to call 9-1-1, but what if she's telling the truth and he does something?"

Tim understood Kevin's frustration. "It's always better to be safe than sorry. Call dispatch and let them know we're heading over there. See if she called the non-emergency line since nothing has come over the radio."

Kevin picked up the handset and called in to the station as Tim turned in the direction of the apartment complex. Dispatch confirmed they hadn't received a call from that address or number. Kevin was tense in the seat next to him, rubbing his palms up and down his thighs.

"This is why you told me not to give out my personal number, isn't it?"

"It's one of the reasons."

"What should I do?"

"Let's see how she acts when we arrive. You may not have to do anything. You may have to be blunt and tell her you're not interested and not to call you anymore."

"Man, I hate confrontation."

Tim's lips quirked up. "Kevin—you're a cop. Confrontation is kind of your job."

"Exactly. It's my job and I can be confrontational with a

suspect if I have to be because that's what I'm supposed to do. I hate personal confrontation. I don't like disappointing people."

"Can't make everyone happy, especially if you're not happy."

"Maybe...but I can pretend to be happy if everyone else is happy."

Tim glanced at his young trainee out of the corner of his eye as he pulled into the apartment complex. Was something else going on in his life that he needed to be concerned about? Personal issues and depression could affect cops on the job, skewing their reactions to certain situations. He'd have to remember to talk to Kevin's next training officer.

He put the car in park and shut off the engine. "Ready?"

Kevin inhaled. "Yeah. Let's get this over with."

They exited the vehicle and followed the path up to the apartment. Kevin followed and Tim understood he didn't want to take the lead. He knocked sharply on the door. Ashley opened it slowly, revealing that she wore a short slinky robe and a lacy bra and panties. As soon as she saw Tim, she straightened up and pulled the robe around her.

"Oh!" She took a step back and glared accusingly at Kevin. "I thought you'd come alone."

"I told you I was on duty," he said.

"I know, but all the other cops ride around by themselves."

"Ma'am, Officer Moore is still in probationary training status. You called him because you were concerned your ex followed you. Can you point to where you think he is?" She'd tried to set Kevin up with the call and he was damned if she was going to get away with it without a warning.

"Well, I don't think he's here anymore," she said sullenly.

Right. "Just to be sure, do you mind stepping outside while we check your apartment?"

She glanced down. "I'm wearing my robe."

"I understand that, ma'am, but to be sure he didn't find a way to break in, I think we'd both feel better after we check your apartment. For your safety." He paused. "Unless you made the call with the intention of luring Officer Moore here to seduce him in some way, in which case I'll be forced to issue a citation for calling in a false police report."

Her mouth fell open. "I didn't call 9-1-1!"

"Ma'am, you called a duly sworn officer of the law, which is the same as prank calling 9-1-1 and carries the same penalties and fines." He was laying it on thick, but it was the least she deserved.

She huffed. "Fine." Holding her robe closed, she shouldered past him onto the walk. "Kevin can wait here with me."

"Actually, Officer Moore needs to accompany me into the apartment." He didn't give her a chance to answer and gestured for Kevin to go ahead of him. "We'll only be a moment."

Closing the door behind them, he grinned.

"Duly sworn officer of the law?" Kevin asked.

"Aren't you?"

"Yes, but who says that?"

Tim shrugged. "Cops on T.V."

He glanced around and walked over to stand next to the small table set with wine glasses and freshly lit candles. "Looks like she had a nice dinner planned for the two of you."

Kevin lifted a lid from a pot on the stove, then covered it back up. "Spaghetti. That would have been a problem."

"You don't like noodles?"

"I'm allergic to tomatoes."

"We can always take her in for attempted murder," Tim said.

Kevin grinned for the first time since he'd answered his phone. "I'll keep that in my back pocket in case she doesn't get the hint."

"Your call. Think she's stewed enough?"

"Let's find out." He took the lead this time and opened the door to a very angry woman.

"What took so long?" she asked. If she'd been wearing shoes, she might have stamped her foot.

"We had to make sure the apartment was secure and that there was no intruder inside."

"Oh my god." Still clutching her robe closed, she pushed past them into the apartment. "No one is hiding in my apartment."

She closed the door partway and stood half behind it. "You can stay for dinner if you'd like," she said, looking at Kevin.

Tim spoke before Kevin could. "We appreciate the offer, ma'am, but we're still on shift and need to get back to real police calls. Next time, if you think your ex is hanging around and you're worried about your safety, call 9-1-1 directly—they will ensure an available car is here quickly."

She glared at him, then shifted her gaze to Kevin. Her eyes and the corners of her mouth softened. "Maybe you could come back after you're done with work."

Kevin cleared his throat. "There's a mandatory briefing after our shift is over and it's going to run really late."

If Tim hadn't been watching so closely, he might have missed the almost imperceptible twitch in the corner of her left eye.

"Tomorrow then." Her voice dripped with annoyance.

"Look, while I'm in training, I don't know how much free time I'm going to have. This really isn't a good time for me." Their radios crackled, followed by a call from dispatch. "We need to go. Have a good evening."

He turned, glanced at Tim, then headed to the patrol car with purpose while talking into the radio mouthpiece on his shoulder.

"Ma'am," Tim said. She slammed the door in his face. He waited until he'd turned his back to the door and couldn't see his face before he smiled.

He slid into the driver side and pulled his seatbelt across his shoulder. "Why didn't you tell her you weren't interested?"

Kevin didn't look up from the department laptop. "I didn't want to hurt her feelings. I just don't want her to keep calling me."

"Hate to say it, but I don't think you've heard the last from her. She seems to have taken a liking to you."

"Yeah…well…she's going to have to find someone else to like." He finished typing. "Store owner reported some vandalism on the back of their building on Market Street."

That was just down from Elba's cafe. His sweet tooth kicked in thinking about the delicious napoleon pastries he'd had the other day at lunch. "Tell you what—after we're done with this call, I'll treat you to a coffee and a pastry."

Kevin rested his elbows on the window ledge and grabbed the oh-shit handle. "Is that a euphemism for a donut?"

"Absolutely not. I never euphemism my pastries."

CHAPTER 12

"*He's definitely worth putting on a to-do list.*"

Zoe hadn't been able to get Denise's words out of her head for the past three days. She'd overheard Gabby tell her in Portuguese she should make a move on Tim. When Zoe had replied she had enough on her to-do list already, Gabby had told her a man was not something you put on a checklist. Denise had caught the gist of what they'd said. When she'd hugged Zoe good-bye, she'd taken the time to whisper, "Tim is a great guy. He's definitely worth putting on a to-do list."

The bell over the door tinkled as it opened. Zoe slid the tray of fresh caramel eclairs onto the shelf of the display case and stood. "Welcome to the Cafe. I'll be— Are you following me?"

It was as if her thoughts had conjured him into Elba's cafe. He really did look good in a uniform. The dark short sleeve shirt hugged his broad shoulders and the utility belt sat perfectly on his lean hips.

A smile tugged at his lips. Damn, why was every encounter she had with him in some way awkward and embarrassing?

"I came in for coffee and pastry. Are you working here now?" He stepped closer to the counter.

"One of Elba's waitresses has morning sickness so I offered to help out for a couple of weeks. I can't do anything with the bookstore until the inspector signs off and it's better than sitting at home staring at my to-do list."

Why the hell had she mentioned her list? Now all she could think of was adding Tim's name to it.

"You okay?" he asked.

"Yes. Why?"

"You looked flushed."

She picked up a napkin and waved it in front of her face. "I just came out of the kitchen. It's hot."

His look was skeptical. "Okay. Zoe, this is my partner Kevin. Kevin, this is my neighbor Zoe."

The younger officer was cute in a very clean-cut, all-American way with his short blond hair and blue eyes. He filled out his uniform almost as nicely as Tim. He was much too young for her —maybe not young enough to be her son, but young enough to be someone she would have babysat in high school.

"It's nice to meet you, ma'am," he held out his hand.

Taking it, she glanced at his name tag. Kevin Moore. No... "Did you used to go by Kev Kev when you were little?"

His eyes widened. "How did you know that?"

"Did you live on Wisteria Place?"

"Yeah. My parents are still there, actually."

"Holy cow! I babysat you in high school."

"Oh wow! I thought you looked a little familiar, but I never would have figured it out." He walked around the counter and pulled her into a big hug. "How are you? Did you move back to the area?"

She stepped out of his embrace. "I'm good. I just moved back. I'm opening a bookstore next door."

He glanced over his shoulder at Tim, flinched a little, and walked back around the counter. Zoe looked at Tim questioningly, but his expression was blank.

"I'll have to let my mom know—she loves to read."

Zoe grinned. "I'm glad that hasn't changed. She was my source for most of my romance novels while I was in high school. So... are you guys staying for coffee and pastry or do you want them to go?"

Kevin looked at Tim.

"We have some time. We can eat here," Tim said.

The door to the kitchen swung open behind them. "Zoe, sweetie, I cannot read your handwriting for the life of me. I know you're a hot Brazilian babe, but I don't read Portuguese."

Rob stopped at the edge of the counter and looked at her expectantly.

"It is not that bad," she said.

He cocked an eyebrow and held the order slip out to her. "Translate, please."

She took the piece of paper from him, held it close, and then moved it farther away. Maybe it wasn't her best penmanship, but she'd been in a rush to get the order in so she could go to the bathroom before her bladder burst.

"Grilled ham and cheese, brioche bread, side salad."

She shoved the order back at him, but his attention was not on her. It was on Kevin and Tim, still standing at the counter. More specifically at Kevin, who was staring equally as hard back at Rob.

"Rob, this is Kevin and Tim. Kevin and Tim, this is Rob—he's the cook."

Rob held out his hand to Kevin. "It's a pleasure to meet one of Haven Springs' finest." His wink was almost comically exaggerated.

Kevin's cheeks were bright red and he had a hard time looking directly at Rob, but he managed to mumble a "Nice to meet you."

"Rob," she said.

"Huh?" He hadn't let go of Kevin's hand and barely turned his head in her direction.

"Food."

"Oh. Right. Ham and cheese. Got it." He took the order and pushed through the swinging door to the kitchen.

"Why don't you guys grab a seat and I'll get you some coffee? Is regular coffee all right or would you like a latte or cappuccino?" she asked.

"Regular for me," Kevin said.

"Same here." Tim led the way to a two-seater table against the back wall.

The back view was as nice as the front view. Jeez, she was as bad as Rob. Taking two cups from the rack, she grabbed the carafe of freshly brewed coffee and took them to their table. Pouring their coffee, she asked, "Do you know what you guys want?"

"Are there any of those napoleon things?" Tim asked.

She glanced over her shoulder at the display case. Elba had been baking that morning before retreating to her office to work on invoices, but Zoe wasn't sure what she'd made. "Let me check in the back. Do you have a backup in case there aren't any?"

"What did you put into the case when we walked in?"

"Caramel eclairs."

His tongue darted out and licked his lips, drawing her gaze to his mouth and his full, kissable lips. Where had that thought come from? She resisted the urge to mimic his action. Barely.

"I'll just take one of those," he said.

She blinked and tore her gaze from him and looked at Kevin. "And for you?"

"I'll have the same," he said.

"Okay. Be right back." No, she wasn't running away, even though it kind of felt that way. She had orders to fill. Food to deliver to tables. Images of full lips to get out of her head.

Returning the carafe to the warmer, she pulled down two plates.

"Psst! Psst! Zoe!"

She glanced over her shoulder toward the kitchen. Rob leaned

84

around the swinging door and gestured for her to come over to him.

"Hang on. Let me serve these eclairs."

"No. Now." He ducked back into the kitchen.

She rolled her eyes but pushed through the door. Rob grabbed her and pulled her to the side before she cleared the threshold.

"*Porra*. My arm doesn't move that way."

"Sorry." He rubbed her shoulder to ease the pain. "Tell me about Kevin. Is he dating anyone?"

"I don't know," she said.

"Find out for me," he said.

"What is this, high school? You find out."

"Not here. If he turned me down I'd be devastated and then I'd burn everyone's order and Elba would fire me."

"That's not overly dramatic at all. How do you know he's even gay?" She was genuinely curious. She'd had her suspicions when he'd been younger, but she'd also chalked it up to him not being a rough-and-tumble kind of kid.

"Oh, sweetie. My gay-dar is perfect. Please? I'll owe you."

"Fine. I'll figure out a way to ask him."

"Thank you! You're my favorite today!" He smushed her face into his chest and shook her side-to-side in a hug.

She pushed against his stomach. "Quit! You're smothering me."

"Sorry." He patted her on the head.

Swatting at his arm, she ducked her head away. "Pat me on the head again and I'm not asking him anything."

"But you're so tiny and adorable. I want to fold you up and stick you in my pocket." He mimed doing exactly what he said, then laughed at her glare.

She went back into the dining room and finished fixing their plates. Tim barely let the plate settle on the table before he cut off a piece and gobbled it up. His eyes closed in ecstasy as he chewed and his tongue darted out to catch a small speck of caramel at the corner of his mouth. It was...very erotic. Watching a guy eat should not be that sexy.

Turning to Kevin, she said, "I know this is very high schoolish, but Rob would like to know if you're seeing anyone." She wasn't going to be subtle after Rob patted her on the head and threatened to make her a pocket elf.

Kevin's gaze darted between her and Tim and his Adam's apple bobbed up and down. "I— Uh— Does he have a sister he wants to set me up with?"

She glanced between him and Tim. "No... He wants to know for himself," she said quietly.

He cleared his throat and looked down at his plate. "Oh. Uh...I'm not—"

Tim leaned forward. "I won't say anything if you're not out." His voice was low and reassuring. "If it's the Department you're worried about, don't be—there's at least three people on the force that are openly out. I was even a groomsman at one of the weddings last year."

Her heart fluttered in her chest. She hadn't considered Kevin might not be out and Tim's immediate acceptance and reassurance assuaged some of the guilt she felt for inadvertently outing him to his partner.

"I appreciate that. It's not the job. My family is very conservative." His voice broke toward the end.

Zoe rubbed Kevin's shoulder. "I'm sorry. I didn't mean to put you on the spot. That was really careless of me."

He squeezed her hand. "It's not your fault. It's not that I'm not out—a few close friends know—but I don't broadcast my personal life from the rooftops."

"I've only known Rob for a couple of weeks, but he's a really nice guy and very genuine. I can give you his number and if you're interested you can give him a call. If not, he'll live. Unless he pats me on the head again, then all bets are off."

At least he smiled at her poor attempt to lighten the mood.

Rubbing his shoulder one last time, she left them to their pastries and made the rounds of the few occupied tables. She filled their cups once and tried to keep an eye on Kevin's mood. She could kick herself for being so careless, especially since it didn't seem that he'd shared with Tim. Less than fifteen minutes later, they stood at the register to pay their bill.

"How were the eclairs?"

"They were delicious," Tim said.

She looked at his lips, because where else would she look when he said it like that? "Would you like some to go?"

"No, thank you. I try to limit my sweets to one a day otherwise I'd never fit into my uniform."

"I don't see that being a problem."

"Why, Miss Acevedo, have you been checking me out?"

His smirk, accompanied by that damn dimple, made her insides gooier than the caramel on the eclairs.

"No," she said forcefully. "I just— You—" She waved her hand vaguely in his direction as if that explained everything that needed explaining. It should.

He winked but thankfully didn't tease her anymore. "Kevin, I'll meet you outside."

Kevin stepped up to the register and handed over his bill and money. "If I could get that other thing you offered as well?"

It took a second for his request to click. "Oh! Yes! Hang on."

She pushed through to the kitchen. "Give me your number now."

"You have my number," Elba said.

"Not you. Rob."

"Really?" he asked.

"Yes. Hurry before he has to leave."

He rattled off his number while bouncing on his toes like a little kid on Christmas morning and she had to bat his hands away and threaten to tear up the note when he tried to pat her on the head again.

CHAPTER 13

Tim trudged down the stairs, pulling a shirt over his head as he went. He'd go for a run after he fed Mitzy. What the hell kind of name was that for a dog? Denise said she'd come with that name, but he had his doubts. He wouldn't put it past her to name a dog Mitzy just to screw with him. He'd tried out other names, but so far none had stuck so he decided to call her "dog"—it wasn't like he was keeping her forever anyway.

When he rounded the corner into his living room, the lady in question raised her head. Upon seeing him, she ambled to her feet and shuffled over. He'd never seen a dog shuffle before, but that was the only way he could think to describe it.

"Come on, girl, outside then I'll get you some food." He didn't bother with a leash since she wasn't going to wander off. Even if she did, as slow as she moved she wouldn't get very far before he caught her. After clearing the back door, she walked exactly six steps into the grass, squatted, and returned to the house.

He filled one bowl with kibble and the other with fresh water. She lay down in front of her food, paws on either side of the bowl, and ate her breakfast.

Hands on his hips, he stared down at her. She paused long

enough to look up at him as if to say "Don't judge me" and went back to eating. Shaking his head, he laced up his running shoes and left out the front. Stretching his quadriceps, movement in his peripheral caught his attention and he glanced to his right.

Zoe appeared to be bouncing on a pogo stick on the far side of her car. It was almost as odd as seeing her stuck in a window. Almost.

It's none of your business. Don't get involved. Right. Telling himself that did not stop him from dropping his leg and crossing their yards to help her. Because he was nothing if not a glutton for punishment.

"What are you doing?" he asked as he rounded the back of her small SUV.

She shrieked and slipped off the tire iron she'd been bouncing on, tumbling to the ground.

"Oh, shit." He crouched down next to her. "Are you okay? Is anything hurt?"

She groaned and sat up. "Just my pride. How do you always manage to find me in the most awkward situations?"

He grinned at her disgruntled tone. "How do you always manage to be in the most awkward situations when I find you?"

"I'm pretty sure they aren't awkward until you show up."

"I'm pretty sure getting stuck in a window was awkward before I showed up."

If glares could kill, he would probably be a pile of ash. Chuckling, he helped her to her feet. "You good?"

"Yes." She dusted off the seat of her pants. Shaking the curls out of her face, she twisted her hair up into some kind of precarious pile on top of her head and secured it with a clip.

A few loose curls escaped and his fingers itched to see if they were as soft as he remembered. "Lug nuts stuck?"

"No, I just enjoy jumping up and down on a tire iron at five in the morning."

"Smart ass." He looked down at the flatter than flat tire. "Looks like you hit a nail or something. Did you notice if it was low yesterday?"

"No, but I also didn't check them when I got home."

She had already pulled the spare and jack out of her car, so he crouched down next to the car, grabbed the tire iron and hefted on it. "Sucker is on there tight."

"Would you like to try jumping on it?"

He grinned up at her. "Are you always this surly in the morning?"

She scrubbed her hands over her face. "Sorry. I'm not a very good morning person, especially when I'm stressed."

"What are you stressed about?" He grunted and the nut finally gave. Turning the iron a few more times for good measure, he moved to the next one.

"The building inspector is coming by the bookstore this morning. I'm nervous we aren't going to pass and if that happens, it's going to cost more money I haven't budgeted for and more time I haven't accounted for."

"Do you have a reason to think you won't pass?" The next two nuts loosened with little effort.

"No. Linda assured me everything is good and in compliance, but it's a big deal and it's not something I can control so I'm freaking out about it."

Finishing the final nut, he set the tire iron aside and grabbed the jack. Peering under the car, he placed it near the back support and raised the car.

"What time is the inspection?" he asked.

"Ten o'clock." She lifted the spare tire off the ground and rolled it closer to him.

Pulling the flat tire off, he set it out of the way and took the new tire from her. "And you're going in now so you can freak out there instead of here?"

"No. I told Elba I would help her out in the cafe this morning so she could train her new waitress."

"Have you guys known each other a while?"

"Almost fifteen years. We were roommates at our first assignment."

"Where was that?"

"Las Vegas, Nevada."

He finger-tightened the nuts and picked up the tire iron. "That must have been a blast."

She held the tire still while he spun the nuts as much as he could with the tire still lifted. "Not really. We were only nineteen so our partying options were limited."

Tossing the tire iron to the side, he eased the jack down and tightened the lug nuts more. "Good as new."

"Thank you. Hopefully it didn't completely ruin your morning."

He gathered up the tools and jack and placed them in the storage bag, returning it to the back of her car. He moved as close as he could to her. "I don't mind helping."

Her gaze dropped. "Do you...uh...tire fix?"

Damn, she was adorable. "You mean where can you take your tire to get it fixed?"

"Um, yes. That."

"I'll take it in for you and get it patched."

Her gaze darted up to his. "You don't have to do that. You already changed it for me."

He gave in and twisted one long curl around his finger. It was as soft as it looked. Her breath caught in her throat and she swallowed hard, staring at his finger out of the corner of her eye as he dragged it down the curl.

"You can treat me to dinner."

"Huh?"

He released the curl and it bounced back into position. "In exchange for taking your tire to get fixed, you can treat me to dinner."

"Oh."

It came out breathy and he wanted to hear it under different circumstances. To feel that soft exhalation against his cheek.

"Okay."

"Okay. Good luck today, Zoe." He winked and took a few steps back. Leaning down, he hefted the tire onto his shoulder and strode across the lawn.

"Thank you," she called out.

"You're welcome." He grinned and tossed the tire into the back of his truck. He waved back at Zoe, still standing beside her car and went inside to take a shower. He wasn't going to get his run in, but for once he wasn't upset about the disruption to his schedule.

TIM GLANCED over his notes for Kevin's training report. He was glad he had nothing but good things to say about his performance. That wasn't always the case and he enjoyed writing positive reports a hell of a lot better than negative ones. Kevin was going to be a good cop and a good addition to the force. He just hoped he got some of his personal issues figured out. Not that he'd put that in his report—Kevin had shared a lot of information with him after they'd left the Cafe the other day and he wouldn't betray his confidence—but he'd be a better cop overall if he didn't have those things hanging over his head.

His phone rang and he answered on the second ring. "Larken."

"Hey, it's Bubba."

Leaning back in his chair, he arched his back to relieve the ache. "Hey. Tire ready?" He'd dropped it off on his way into work.

"Where'd you get that tire?"

He leaned forward. "My neighbor. Helped her change it this morning, why?"

"Someone have it out for her?"

"Not that I know of. Why?"

"Tire was slashed, man. Was that the only tire that was flat?"

What the fuck? "Yeah. The other three were fine."

"Might want to have her take her car in to have them checked out. Unusual for a slashed tire to not go flat, but stranger things have happened. Stranger that someone would be pissed off enough to hit one tire, but not the rest of them."

"I'll give her a call."

"You do that. Want me to put a new tire on the rim?"

"Yeah, thanks. I'll pick it up this afternoon."

"Sure thing." Bubba hung up and Tim set his own phone down.

Grabbing his cell phone from the desk, he thumbed through the contacts until he came to the number Denise had texted him. It went to voicemail after only one ring. Either she was already busy with the inspection or she didn't answer unknown numbers. He glanced at the clock. Almost ten o'clock. She might still be at the restaurant—he'd try to catch her there.

Pulling up an internet search engine, he typed the Cafe and address into the search bar, then used his work phone to call the number listed.

"Thank you for calling the Cafe. This is Elba."

"Hi, Elba. This is Tim."

Silence answered him.

"Hello? Elba? Are you there?"

"Yes! Sorry. I must have accidentally muted the phone."

"Is Zoe there?"

"You just missed her—she went next door a few minutes ago. Can I take a message?"

"Actually, I realized I don't have her store number. Would you be able to give it to me?"

"And what would you do with her number if I gave it to you?"

He smiled and twirled a pen around his fingers. "I would call her."

"And what would you say to her when you called her?"

"You're being awfully nosy, Elba."

"I'm her best friend. I'm supposed to be nosy."

"Are you going to give me the number?" He wasn't going to tell Elba the real reason he was calling until he talked to Zoe. She could think what she wanted. Not that he wouldn't use Zoe's number to ask her out as well, but that wasn't what he needed it for right now.

"I suppose. Ready?"

"Yup." He typed the number into his cell phone, thanked her and hung up, immediately pressing dial on his cell.

"Book Haven."

"Zoe?"

"Yes."

"This is Tim. Your neighbor." He wasn't sure why he needed to clarify which Tim he was—how many could she possibly know?

"Oh. Hi. Is everything all right?"

"No. Yes. Maybe."

"Well, that's not confusing at all."

Her sarcastic tone made him smile, the same way it had that morning. It wasn't as biting as Denise's, but still got her point across. "Do you know of any reason why someone would slash your tire?"

"What?"

"Because you didn't run over a nail."

She was quiet for a few moments. Could she really be thinking that hard about who would want to slash her tire?

"Not unless Mrs. Wilson is still mad for that time my brother glued her mailbox closed."

His bark of laughter caught him by surprise. "Why—? Never mind, I don't really want to know. I don't think Mrs. Wilson has it out for you for something that happened close to twenty years ago."

"Then no. I have no idea. Could it have been random?"

"Maybe, but it's unusual to have that kind of vandalism

without trying to break into the car or steal the tires. Did you notice any other damage?"

"No, that was all."

"All right. The tire shop is putting a new tire on the rim for you. I'll pick it up and drop it off this evening."

"Um, tonight won't work. I managed to get the internet and phone companies scheduled for this evening and I'm going to get some boxes out of storage so I can start clearing it out and Linda's daughter is going to prep the loft tonight so she can start painting first thing tomorrow and I need to push out job notifications to hire employees and—"

"So you're saying your busy tonight?"

"Yeah. You can leave it beside the garage."

"I'll hang onto it for ransom."

"Ransom for what?"

"Dinner." He hung up as she sputtered her response, chuckling as he pictured her face at his statement. Dinner could wait a few days while Zoe got her store settled, but he wasn't going to let her off the hook.

CHAPTER 14

T im yawned so hard his jaw cracked and he moved it back and forth. Damn, he hated late night call outs. He pulled onto his street and parked the cruiser behind his truck. Haven Springs wasn't big enough and didn't have enough crime for them to have a full mid-shift, but it did mean they rotated being on call for two weeks at a time, which meant he got to drive the company car for the week. Who said this job didn't have its perks? Thankfully, he'd be able to go in a few hours late tomorrow since he'd responded to the call.

He glanced over at Zoe's house and saw her car in the driveway. She'd still been gone when he'd left to respond to the fender bender. Now, close to midnight, her car was there but the dome light was on. Either she didn't close her door all the way or she'd forgotten to turn it off when she went inside.

Did she have one of those cars that would die if the dome light was on? Oh, hell. He'd make sure her door was closed all the way at least. If it was and the car was locked, he'd check that she had a way to jump her car in the morning. If nothing else, he'd make sure his battery charger was good to go and accessible for her tomorrow.

Her car door wasn't closed all the way, so he shut it firmly. On the way back to his house, he passed the front door, stopped, and backed up.

What the hell?

He pulled his pistol from his belt and quietly approached her front door. It was ajar—with the keys still dangling from the lock.

Stopping right on the threshold, he leaned forward and cocked his ear toward the opening, listening for any noise from inside. Met with only silence, he used his left hand to slowly push the door open. The small foyer was empty and he walked into the living room.

"Fuck."

He swept the room and knelt down next to Zoe's body, face down on the floor of her living room. There was no obvious bleeding. He found her carotid and continued to scan the room while he checked her pulse. It beat strong and steady under his fingers. She shifted and pulled her arms into her body, tucking them close into her chest with a sigh.

"Zoe?" He shook her shoulder. "Are you all right?"

"Sleep," she mumbled.

He dropped to a knee and cradled his head in his free hand. "For fuck's sake."

Holstering his gun, he shook Zoe harder. "Zoe, wake up."

She swatted in his direction. "Leave me alone."

He sniffed hard but didn't smell any alcohol. Had she really fallen asleep on the floor? With her front door wide open? Fucking hell.

"Zoe, you need to wake up."

"Those books don't go there." She rolled to her side and tucked her hands under her head.

Tim scrubbed his hands through his hair.

"Come on, Sleeping Beauty, upstairs." He slid his arms under her shoulders and knees and stood. She tucked her head into the crook of his neck. Anger and worry warred with exasperation. What the fuck was she thinking? Yes, it was a safe neighborhood, but she shouldn't be leaving her doors open.

Flipping the light on at the bottom of the stairs, he carried her upstairs into her bedroom and laid her on the bed.

"No pants." Standing up, she unbuttoned her jeans and pushed them down her hips. She lost her balance and leaned over the bed while supporting herself with a hand. Alternating legs, she pulled them out of the legs of her pants. She grabbed the hem of her t-shirt and lifted it to her ribs.

"Okay, no." Tim grasped her hands and put them back at her sides. The glimpse of her high-cut, lace-trimmed underwear was enough. "In bed."

"'Kay." She crawled onto the bed without pulling down the covers.

She didn't have a lot of extra pillows or blankets on her bed, so he reached over and pulled the comforter over the top of her. She yanked the edge of the blanket over her shoulder and adjusted her pillow.

Tim stared down at her in the dim light from the hall. Who the hell slept that hard? He pivoted sharply and strode out of her room and down the stairs. He pulled her keys from the lock and set them on the table next to the door. Thumbing the lock, he left the house and pulled the door behind him. He stopped just before it latched.

"Damn it." He pushed the door open, grabbed her keys from the table, and then pulled the door closed behind him.

What if she had been drinking? He hadn't smelled alcohol, but she was pretty short—a couple of drinks could have put her over the limit without her smelling like booze. What if she drove home intoxicated? So many things could have happened. She could have killed herself or someone else. Because really, who slept that hard without taking something?

He stopped, turned, and looked back at her house. What the fuck was he doing? Visions of Bree covered in blood flashed through his mind. He knew exactly what he was doing—preventing another woman from being attacked. It was irresponsible, never mind unsafe, for her to have done that. There was no excuse for it.

He turned to his house, took a step, stopped and turned back to Zoe's house, then spun again to his house. He was making himself dizzy. It wasn't any of his business. He needed to stay out of it. He needed to stay away from women who needed to be saved. She might not be like Monica had been, but he was fighting an overwhelming urge to protect her, which history told him was a bad thing. It wasn't his job.

Growling in frustration, he continued to his house, unlocked the door, and took the stairs two at a time. In his room, he tossed his uniform on his bed, not bothering to hang it up like he normally did.

He was a cop. It was his job. Zoe needed to understand the danger she'd put herself in. Anything could have happened. Anyone could have walked into her house and attacked her. Then what? He was going to go back over there, wake her ass up, and describe in all the gory details what could have happened.

He stomped down the stairs, ready to put his plan into action, except the dog was sitting at the bottom waiting for him. She did some strange half warble, half howl at him as he hit the bottom step.

"You need out? Come on. Let's go." He slapped the side of his thigh and led her to the back door, sliding it open for her.

Instead of going outside, she lay down and rested her head on his feet—something she'd never done before.

"What are you waiting for? Go outside." He gestured toward the door. She didn't move, only licked her chops and moved her head closer to his ankles.

"Seriously? I need to go."

She let out a pitiful moan and heaved a sigh. Tim dropped his head back and stared at the ceiling. Looking down at her again, he said, "Do you need attention? Is that it? Come on."

He eased his feet out from under her chin and sat in closest dining room chair. She rolled up to a stand, shuffled over to him, and dropped her hip on his foot, resting her head on his knee.

"What's up with you?" He scratched behind her ear and his thoughts turned to Zoe, asleep in her bed. What was he supposed to do? Yeah, he could wake her up and yell at her, but what good would it do? He wanted her to understand the danger she'd been in, but at the same time did he want to get that personal with a woman again?

What would he do if he'd found Mrs. Wilson like that? He would have helped her to bed, locked up, and approached her in the morning to let her know what she'd done was unsafe. Granted, he would have averted his eyes had Mrs. Wilson taken her pants off instead of appreciating the way the lace edge of Zoe's panties framed the round globes of her ass, but that was beside the point. He would have made sure Mrs. Wilson was safe and understood the mistake she'd made.

So that's what he'd do with Zoe. To be sure he didn't miss her in the morning, he'd sleep on her couch. That way he could be sure he didn't miss her before one of them left for the day.

Mitzy stood and returned to her dog bed.

Tim lifted an eyebrow. "Was that all you wanted?" he asked.

If dogs had expressions like people did, Mitzy would be giving him a "you're a dumbass" look. Oddly, he wasn't as angry as he'd been when he'd stormed through his door. Taking the time to pet the dog had given him chance to calm down and think about the situation with Zoe instead of storming back over there and causing a scene. That would not have been the best situation, nor would it have led to the best outcome. He wanted Zoe to understand the danger she'd been in without pissing her off.

"Are you some sort of witch dog?"

Mitzy groaned and rolled to her side, apparently done with their conversation. That was fine with him. He had a couch to go get comfortable on.

CHAPTER 15

Zoe stretched, pointing and flexing her toes. She blinked open her eyes and looked at the alarm clock next to her bed. Seven-twenty-nine. It was nice not having to get up at the crack of dawn to help Elba. She loved her, but those hours were brutal.

Flicking the alarm off before it could beep, she stretched one last time and threw the covers back. Weird, she'd only pulled the covers over herself last night without getting under them.

Wow, she'd slept hard. She didn't even remember climbing into bed. Hell, she barely remembered getting home. All the little things she'd meant to take care of quickly had ended up taking more time than she expected. At least now they were out of the way and she could focus on all the big things she needed to do. First thing would be hiring some employees so when all the books started arriving, she had some help.

She twisted her back to work out a couple of kinks. Ugh. Apparently she'd been so tired all she'd managed to do was take her pants off. Reaching under the back of her shirt, she unhooked her bra and peeled it off through the armholes, then rubbed where the underwire had dug into the soft skin under her breasts.

Not bothering with pants, she went downstairs to fix a cup of coffee before she got in the shower and got ready for the day. Rounding the corner into the living room, she froze.

Someone was on her couch.

The top of a man's head was just visible on the armrest. With the back of the couch facing her, there was no way to tell who the head belonged to.

Glancing over her shoulder, she judged the distance to the door and noted the bolt was thrown. How many seconds would it take to throw the lock, open the door, and race next door to Tim's? She took a careful step back, wincing when her heel landed on a loose part of the floor.

"I already heard you upstairs, so you may as well come in."

"*Puta merda!*" All the air left her lungs in a whoosh and she realized she'd been holding her breath. Resting her hand on her chest, she felt her heart pounding against her sternum as the adrenaline receded.

"What are you doing in my house?"

Tim stood up from the couch and stalked toward her. Worry returned and she backed away from him until she hit the wall behind her.

He was angry—she could see it in the scowl on his face—but there was something else in his eyes as well.

He stopped a couple of feet away from her. "I'm in your house because when I got home from a call-out last night, your car door was open. Then I saw your front door was wide open and the keys were still in the lock. When I found you passed out on the floor of your living room, I thought you'd been attacked and left for dead."

Her heart fluttered for completely different reasons than fear. He'd been worried about her. That was why he was so angry.

"Were you drunk?"

Her brows snapped together. "What?"

"Drunk. I didn't smell any alcohol—had you been drinking?"

"Of course not! I wouldn't drive if I'd been drinking. I was tired."

"So tired you didn't have the energy to close and lock your door? So tired you didn't wake up when I shook you or carried you upstairs to your bed?"

"Yes. I'm a heavy sleeper—I've been known to have complete, lucid conversations with people and not remember them later on —and last night I was exhausted. Between helping Elba out yesterday morning and trying to take care of some things for the store, I'd been going non-stop for more than eighteen hours. I barely remember getting home and going to bed."

"You didn't go to bed, I put you in bed."

She pulled down the front hem of her t-shirt, conscious of the fact that it and her underwear were all she wore. "I'm not wearing any pants."

Of course he looked, because what man wouldn't look when a woman pointed out she didn't have on any pants?

"You insisted on taking them off before you got in bed."

"And you didn't see anything?"

He crossed his arms and rocked back on his heels. "I might have caught a glimpse."

"A glimpse?"

His arms went up in surrender. "Don't blame me. I had to fight you to keep your shirt on."

"You could have left the room," she said.

"I wanted to make sure you got into your bed and didn't fall asleep on the floor again."

She looked down and bit the corner of her lip. "I laid down on the floor because my back hurt. I remember thinking I'd rest for a few minutes before going upstairs."

His bare feet bracketed hers and she could feel his heat on her front.

"You worried me, Zoe."

Her gazed moved up to his chest. "I didn't mean to. It didn't occur to me that anyone would."

"You were married. Didn't your ex ever worry about you?"

She shrugged. "Not really."

"Then he was an idiot. That probably goes without saying since he let you go."

He hadn't let her go so much as shoved her out the door, but she wasn't going to share that with Tim. She wasn't sure what was going on, but this felt like a "moment." The kind that she'd only read about because "moments" didn't happen in real life.

"Zoe."

"Yeah?"

His hand rose slowly and he used his fingers to lift her chin and tilt her head back. She kept her gaze lowered until she had no choice except to close her eyes or look up.

"I'm going to kiss you now."

"Oh."

His full lips tilted up ever so slightly. "Oh."

She ended up closing her eyes anyway. His lips were soft on hers—a bare whisper of pressure as his tongue touched the center of her bottom lip. She gasped and his mouth settled fully on hers. He was gentle until she touched her tongue to his.

He grasped the back of her head and groaned. His head came down until it was almost even with hers, then he wrapped one arm around her back and lifted her so she was level with him.

It was so much better when she didn't have to crane her neck to kiss him. She wrapped her arms around his neck and her legs around his waist. The door was against her back and his arm had moved under her ass. His erection cradled between her thighs sent a shiver racing through her body. His hand edged under her shirt, branding the skin under her breast. When he palmed her and ran a thumb over her erect nipple, tiny bolts of electricity coursed through her body. Groaning, she squeezed her legs, trying to get even closer.

His hand slid back to her waist and she whimpered with disappointment. He eased off the kiss and rested his forehead against hers. His breath fanned across her swollen mouth, tightening the sensitive skin on her lips as the moisture dried.

"I didn't mean to do that," he said.

"You said you were going to kiss me."

"Yeah, but I didn't mean for it to go as far as it did."

"Oh."

He lifted his head. "That doesn't sound like a good 'oh.'"

"No, it is, it's just— I, uh—" She was disappointed that he'd stopped, but didn't want to tell him that when he was the one who'd slowed things down. "Um, you can put me down."

"No."

"No?"

"I'm going to keep you here until you tell me why you're upset."

"You can't keep me here." She wiggled, trying to get down, but that only made his erection nestle closer to her center.

His eyes darkened and his gaze dropped to her mouth. "I like you here. Besides, what are you going to do? Call the cops?"

She glared at him. "Fine. *Esse foi o beijo mais quente da minha vida e eu não queria que você parasse.* Happy?"

"I didn't understand a word of that," he said, shaking his head.

"It's not my fault you don't speak Portuguese. You said tell you —you didn't specify which language I had to use."

He closed the distance between them and kissed her hard. Maybe he'd gotten the gist of it, but no, he stopped again. "I'm letting you go on a technicality."

He stepped back and her legs dropped from his waist before he let her slide down his body. "How busy are you going to be this weekend?"

"Why?"

"Curiosity."

Curiosity for why? "I'm not sure. I'm going to spend Saturday and Sunday interviewing applicants and Elba said something about going out Friday night to celebrate."

"Where does she plan on going Friday?"

"Some country bar in Raleigh she likes to go to."

"City Limits?" he asked.

"Sounds familiar. Why?"

"There's a couple of bars you should avoid—wanted to make sure it wasn't one of those."

"Elba does not like to slum, so I'm sure it's not one of those."

His gaze raked down her body and she would have sworn he growled low in his throat. "I need to go to work. If you're going to be really late tonight, call me and let me know so I can make sure you get home okay."

She shook her head. "You don't have to do that."

"I'm doing it anyway. Call me, Zoe." He stared down at her, his hazel eyes searching hers.

"All right."

His grin showed off his dimple. "Thank you."

He left her with a too-brief kiss and weak knees. She hadn't been lying when she'd told him that had been the hottest kiss of her life. Granted, he hadn't understood what she'd said but that didn't make it any less true. Some part of her mind said his protectiveness should annoy her, that he was just another *machismo* guy with too much testosterone like her brother and her ex, but it was different. It wasn't as if he was trying to control what she did, only that he wanted to make sure she was safe while she did it. She wasn't ashamed to say she liked it. It didn't feel like he was being patronizing or condescending—it felt like he cared.

It was…nice. She didn't have an issue with being taken care of. At least, not in the sense that she was helpless or wanted someone to provide for her, but having a guy who worried and wanted to make sure she was safe…? Yeah…that was hot.

Leaning against the door, she sighed and looked at the checklist tacked to her wall. Right. Coffee and a to-do list. She might not have added Tim to her list, but she had a feeling he'd just added himself.

CHAPTER 16

Zoe locked the door of the bookstore and used the key Elba
had given her to unlock the door of the Cafe. Making sure
to throw the bolt again, she made her way through the dim dining
room and pushed through the swinging door into the kitchen.
"Elba? You back here?"

She poked her head out of her office. "Hey. I just need to finish
up this paperwork and then we can go." She disappeared back into
the office. "I brought my clothes with me so I can get ready at
your house. Hope that's okay."

Edging behind Elba, Zoe flopped down into the oversized
armchair in the corner of the office. The space really wasn't big
enough for more than one person at a time.

"I'm not sure I'm up for going out tonight."

Elba's shoulders dropped and she spun her desk chair to face
her. "Zoe, you promised."

"El, I'm too tired to go out tonight. Can't we celebrate some
other time?"

"This is the only weekend April is staying with Jackassasaurus
for the next two months and I know you'll be too busy then with
the bookstore by then to really have a good time." She clasped her

hands under her chin as if praying and batted her eyelashes. "Pleeeeaaaasssse?"

Zoe dropped her head to the back of the chair and stared at the ceiling tiles. *"Por que eu aguento você?"*

"Because I'm beautiful and charming and you love me?"

She lifted her head. "Did you understand that?"

Elba shook hers. "No, but I figured it had to be something along the lines of questioning why you love me."

"Something like that." She sighed. "Fine, but we're not staying out all night, we're not doing any shots, and you have to help me weed through applications tomorrow afternoon."

"Deal!" Elba held out her hand to shake on it. "But you have to dress up."

Zoe squinted at her. "Define 'dress up.'"

TIM POKED at his grilled chicken and glanced at the clock on the stove. He had no plans other than his usual dinner and game shows. It was Friday night and he was at home. Alone. Normally he had no issue with his routine—he enjoyed his routine—but nothing had been normal since Zoe had moved next door. She was like a little dirt devil—just enough force to cause some chaos, but not so much that it destroyed everything in its path.

That kiss. That kiss had been anything but normal. He shouldn't have touched her but she'd looked so sexy with her hair wild from sleep and her bare legs for days. He was surprised it had taken him as long as it did before he kissed her. At least he'd given her a chance to say no by warning her first.

She hadn't said no. She'd kissed him back. She'd wrapped her legs around his waist and it had taken all of his strength and willpower to stop touching her and put her down. All day he'd thought about "dropping by" the bookstore to see if she needed any help, but it would have been an excuse to see her. He'd even turned down Jase's offer to go out to the campsite for the weekend, something he always looked forward to, because in the back of his mind was the knowledge that Zoe was out tonight.

City Limits wasn't a rough bar like The Deck, but it sure as hell was a meat market. Some of the younger officers in the department talked about how easy it was to pick up women at the bar, especially when they mentioned they were cops.

He tore into the last couple bites of his chicken. The idea of any man trying to pick up Zoe had him seeing green. Taking his plate back into the kitchen, he tossed it into the sink without bothering to wash it. In the living room, he propped his feet up on the large footstool and flipped through the channels, trying to find something to watch. Only when he'd gone through the entire channel lineup twice without remembering anything he'd seen did he give up and throw the remote on the couch next to him.

He sighed and looked at Mitzy. "What should I do? Sit here like some loser or try to find her at the bar like some loser?"

She sighed and let out a long, whistling fart.

"Bar it is."

Dress up meant a black, knee-length wrap dress and sling-back wedges. It was the only thing she owned that Elba deemed going out appropriate without having to go shopping for new clothes. Zoe had managed to talk her out of that since they were both keeping to a budget.

She leaned close to Elba as they made their way to the bar. "This place is a meat market."

"Exactly." Elba leaned over the edge of the bar, showing off her cleavage to the bartender. The move caught his attention and he smiled at her.

"What can I get for you?"

"Two vodka sodas with a splash of cranberry juice."

"Sure thing." He made of show of mixing the drinks by flipping the vodka bottle before pouring the alcohol into a shaker cup.

Zoe poked Elba in the rib. "Looks like you've got a fan."

She leaned back from the bar. "He's entirely too young, but it's fun to flirt."

"Do you ever go home with anyone?" Zoe asked.

"Hell, no. I don't pick up guys and I don't get picked up."

The bartender slid their drinks to them. "Eleven dollars, ladies."

Elba passed a couple bills across the bar with a wink. "Thanks, sweetie."

"Why are we here if you aren't picking anyone up?" Zoe asked.

El turned and surveyed the crowd around the oval-shaped dance floor. "Because I like to dance and aside from having really cute butts, country boys know how to two-step. Occasionally I manage to find one that knows how to salsa as well, which pretty much makes my night."

Tilting her head toward an empty high-top table near the dance floor, she said, "Come on. Let's sit so I can see who the best dancers are."

"I can't even remember the last time I went to a bar." Zoe took a sip of her drink. "Whoa. The bartender definitely liked you."

Elba grinned and sipped her drink. "Yeah, he did."

"Excuse me, ladies." A guy in well-worn faded jeans and a t-shirt tipped his baseball cap up, then settled it back in place. "I was hoping one of you would like to dance."

Elba set her glass down. "I'd love to. Watch my drink." She didn't wait for a response before offering her hand to the guy and following him onto the dance floor.

Watching her friend dance around the floor, Zoe finished the last of her drink and eye-balled Elba's. As the song transitioned into another fast-paced tune, Elba passed and flashed her a smile. Setting her glass down, she picked up the other one since Elba wasn't going to be returning anytime soon. She'd buy the next round to make up for it.

"You two-fisting tonight?"

An arm slid around the back of her chair and she turned to face her companion who leaned on the table, effectively boxing her in.

"Are you stalking me now?" She let her gaze travel down his body. He was dressed in much the same way he'd been when she'd seen him at the market a few weeks ago, except now he wore a light blue button-down shirt, the sleeves rolled back to expose his forearms. She struggled to feign indifference at his arrival when all she wanted to do was run her fingers through the dusting of dark hair on his arms.

Tim smirked. "Is it stalking if you told me where you'd be?"

"It is if you weren't invited."

"Sounds like you should file a report with the police. I know a guy."

She smiled at his teasing tone. "I should probably get his number if you're going to continue to be a nuisance."

He clutched his chest. "I can't believe you think I'm a nuisance after all the times I've helped you."

"Hmm. I suppose you have helped me out with a couple of things."

The corner of one eyebrow rose.

"Okay, yes. You've been very helpful. I swear I'm not usually so accident prone."

"You do seem to be having a particularly bad streak of luck." He picked up her empty glass and tipped an ice cube into his mouth, crunching on it.

"Would you like a drink," she asked.

"I drove. I'll get a water in a few minutes."

"Are you on call?"

He shook his head. "No, just don't drink that much."

"Is it because you...?" Well, shit. How did she ask if he had a drinking problem?

"I'm not an alcoholic," he said, guessing what she failed to articulate.

"Why don't you drink?"

"I've seen what it can do to people when they've had too much. I enjoy the occasional beer during a game or when the family barbecues, but that's all."

"Were you ever in the military?"

He shook his head. "No. I knew I wanted to serve, but I knew I didn't want to be in the military. Cop was the next best thing."

She tilted her head. "Why didn't you want to be in the military?"

"My dad was in the Army—Special Forces. He was gone a lot and I was old enough to see how it affected my mom. It wasn't only the constant moving, it was the constant worry. I remember the look of fear she had every time someone knocked on the door while he was gone. I swore I'd never make someone go through that if I could help it."

She swirled her drink with the straw. "Aren't you in danger as a police officer?"

"Yes, but not nearly as much as I would be in a bigger city. Haven Springs has had its fair share of excitement, but it's nothing like Raleigh."

Crossing her legs, she saw his gaze drop down and followed where he was looking. Her skirt had fallen open, exposing a wide expanse of thigh. Under normal circumstances, she'd cover up but she liked that Tim was looking. She felt sexy. Desirable.

His thumb brushed the skin between her shoulder blades and her heart kicked against her ribs. His eyes came back to hers. She licked her suddenly dry lips and his gaze dropped to her mouth.

He leaned forward, grazing the corner of her mouth with his lips as he moved closer to her ear. Her eyes fluttered as she caught a whiff of his cologne, the musky scent subtle and sexy.

"Dance with me."

Blinking, she realized the DJ had changed to a slow song. She could only nod.

He dropped his arms and held out his hand, helping her down from the tall stool. Even in her four-inch wedges, she barely reached his chin. Leading her to the middle of the dance floor he stopped and gathered her close, wrapping his right arm tight around her back and using his left to tuck their hands between their bodies. Her other hand rested on his upper arm.

The last time she'd danced with a man had been at her wedding and all she and Mark had done was sway side to side like it was junior high. She knew the basics of a two-step but had always felt awkward dancing with someone she didn't know, even before she got married. Tim had no such issue and led her smoothly around the dance floor, using gentle pressure on her lower back to direct her around other couples. It was effortless and she relaxed as she let him guide her.

As the tension left her body, her focus shifted to other things. The heat of his body. The pressure of his fingers at the base of her spine. His warm breath against her cheek. The slight brush of his lips at the corner of her own. She turned her head so their mouths were closer, the barest space separating them. Neither of them closed the distance.

Her stomach rolled. She'd read somewhere that desire sometimes felt like nausea but had never experienced it. Not until that moment. She was breathless and lightheaded. Her blood raced through her veins and heat pooled in her core. It was the most sensual thing she'd ever felt and all he'd done was dance with her.

"Would you two get a room already?"

Zoe snapped out of her reverie. She and Tim looked at Elba, dancing by with a different guy.

"You two are going to burn down the place if you don't leave. Z, call me later." She danced off with her partner.

Tim hadn't relaxed his hold and she had to lean back against his arm to be able to tilt her head enough to look at him. If he hadn't been holding her, her knees might have buckled from the intensity of his gaze.

"I'd like to take you home, Zoe."

"Okay."

CHAPTER 17

Turning the corner onto their street, Tim glanced at Zoe in the passenger seat of his truck. She had her hands in her lap and was picking at her nails. He couldn't tell whether she was nervous or anxious. Passing his house, he pulled in behind her car and shifted into park.

"It's okay if you've changed your mind," he said.

Zoe looked down at her hands then unbuckled her seat belt.

He tried not to let his disappointment show, but fuck, he was so hard he could feel the seam of his jeans pressing into his dick.

Instead of giving him excuses, telling him goodnight and climbing out of his truck, she climbed on him. Straddling him, she took his hands and placed them on her thighs and guided them under her skirt until he gripped the fleshy part of her hips.

A low groan escaped when she shifted and rubbed her hot core against his crotch.

"What are you doing, Zoe?"

Her fingers ran along the sides of his face, down his neck, and stopped at the collar of his shirt. "What I wanted to do since we got in your truck."

"Sit on my lap and drive me crazy?"

"Yes." She unbuttoned his shirt enough to move her hands to his chest. "I shouldn't. I have too much going on. Too many things on my to-do list. I don't have time to get involved with anyone, but you're so…"

"So what?"

"So everything." She meshed her mouth with his, sliding her tongue in to tangle with his.

He dug his fingers deeper into her lush ass and pulled her closer, lifting his hips to grind up into her. She moaned and rolled her hips.

Breaking the kiss, he had to tilt his head back to avoid her mouth. "We need to go inside, Zoe."

"Do we?"

All he wanted to do was unzip his pants, shove her panties aside, and bury himself deep. "Yes. I don't want to give the neighbors a show."

She dropped her forehead to his and her chest rose and fell as she struggled to compose herself.

Giving her a firm squeeze, he slid his hands out from under her skirt. "Grab your purse, beautiful, and hop out."

The look she gave him made him question his sanity, but their first time wasn't going to be a quick fuck in the front seat of his vehicle. He'd at least get her in the front door of her house before he got her naked.

She picked up her small purse from the console and he opened his door, helping her dismount him and slide out of the truck. He beeped the locks and followed her to the front door, watching the skirt of her dress swish in time with the sway of her hips. The simple dress accentuated her hourglass figure.

Once inside, she tossed her keys into a bowl on a table in the small entryway while he threw the locks on her door. When he turned around, she stood at the bottom of the stairs. Using the banister for balance, she lifted one foot and slipped off a shoe. Instead of placing her foot back on the ground, she stepped onto the first step, lifted her other foot, and slipped off that shoe. Walking backward up the steps, she slowly pulled at the tie of her dress.

Tim kicked off his boots at the bottom of the stairs. Matching her step for step, he unbuttoned the rest of his shirt and followed her up.

She unfastened something on the inside of her dress and shrugged it off, leaving it where it fell.

The sight of Zoe in her simple black bra and panty set made him miss a step and stumble.

"Careful," she said. "It would suck if you fell down the stairs."

"Jesus, woman. You're killing me."

He stripped out of his shirt and unbuckled his belt. Unbuttoning his pants and shoving them down his hips, he decided to sit on a step to take off his jeans rather than risk falling down the stairs. When he turned around, the only sign of Zoe was her satin bra on the upstairs landing.

He scrambled to pull his wallet out of the back pocket of his jeans and grabbed a condom, tucking it into the waistband of his underwear, then followed the short hallway to her bedroom.

She waited at the end of her bed, arms crossed over her chest. Whether to tease him or because she was suddenly shy, he didn't know. His gaze devoured her as he walked toward her. From her full breasts spilling out of her hands to the indent of her waist to the full curve of her hips. His cock pulsed and strained against the confines of his boxer briefs.

He skimmed his hands over her shoulders, down her upper arms, to her hips. His thumbs brushed over her hip bones and he felt the shiver run through her.

"You're beautiful," he said.

"*Tu também.*"

"Do you always speak in Portuguese when you're nervous?"

"Or angry. Or if I want to swear without someone understanding me."

He hooked his fingers into the waistband of her underwear and slid his hands to her ample backside. Pulling her close, he bent and scraped his teeth against the column of her throat, thrilling at her sharp inhalation.

She grasped his shoulders and dropped her head back.

"How do you say you're so fucking sexy?"

"*Você é muito gostoso.*"

He dropped to his knees and sat on his heels. Putting his mouth on the juncture of her thighs, he tongued her through the thin material her panties. He could smell her desire and his dick throbbed in anticipation.

"How do you say I can't wait to taste you?"

"*Eu não posso esperar para sabor tu.*" Her voice was breathless.

Grasping the sides of her panties, he pulled them down her hips and thighs, running his hands down the backs of her calves to help her step out of them. He slid his hands up the front of her legs. When he reached her closely shaven pussy, he traced her seam with his thumbs and she pulsed against him.

He replaced his thumbs with his tongue, delving into her hot, wet center.

Zoe's knees buckled and she fell back against the bed. That worked for Tim. He lifted her legs onto his shoulders and pushed her farther back on the bed. Her hips rose to meet his mouth, her hands clenching in his hair. He circled and flicked her clit with his tongue. Taking his cues from her response, he found the rhythm she liked, keeping a steady pace until her cries became frantic and her heels dug into his back. She shoved her hips at him and grasped the back of his head, holding him in an iron grip with her thighs until she came with a shout.

Tim used the flat of his tongue to keep pressure on her clit as she rode out her orgasm. When the tension left her body and she relaxed her hold on him, he gave her one final, long lick that caused her entire body to shudder.

He wiped his mouth and stood, staring at the gorgeous woman

spread out before him. There was nothing more resplendent than a sexually satisfied woman.

Zoe pushed up and sat at the edge of the bed. "You're wearing entirely too many clothes."

It was his turn to lick his lips. He wanted to feel her mouth on him. Wanted to feel her wet tongue tease him and taste him. At the same time, he hoped she didn't because when he lost himself in her, he wanted to do it in her hot, wet, tight pussy.

She stood up and shoved her fingers between the elastic band and his skin at the back of his waist. Their height difference put her mouth almost level with his chest. She took advantage and flicked her tongue against one nipple.

Tim hissed when she bit down on it. Not hard, but it surprised him. It felt good. Better than he expected.

She pressed her tongue against the nipple then moved her head to the other one. She licked it but paused. "Yes or no?"

He palmed her breasts, hefting their weight. "Definitely yes."

She gasped against his chest when he tweaked her nipples. Keeping her gaze on his, she opened her mouth wide and scraped her teeth against his chest. When she got to his nipple, she sucked hard instead of biting it.

Fuck. He was going to come in his shorts if she kept her mouth on him.

"On the bed, Zoe," he demanded.

The only thing that stopped him from picking her up and throwing her into the center was her look of confusion. Gone was the confident, satisfied woman. In her place was a woman unsure and quickly becoming bashful.

He grasped the back of her head and kissed her. Thrusting his tongue into her mouth until she responded to him with equal heat.

"I want to fuck you, Zoe. I want to bury my cock in your tight pussy and make you scream my name. If you keep teasing me with your mouth I'm not going to be able to do that because I'm going to come in my shorts like I'm a thirteen-year-old boy who got to touch his first pair of tits."

"Oh."

He smirked. "Oh. On the bed."

"One thing first."

Before he knew what she was doing, she'd shoved his briefs down his hips, dropped to her knees, and pulled him between her lips.

"Fuck!" He gave in to the heady feel of her mouth as she sucked him but too soon he felt the tingle in balls that told him he was close to blowing his load.

He grasped her jaw and pulled away until all she could do was lick the slit of his cock.

"On the bed, naughty girl."

She stared at his dick jutting in her face and he almost gave in to the temptation.

He stooped down, scooped her up in his arms, and tossed her onto the center of the bed. Making quick work of pushing his underwear down his legs, he grabbed the condom from the floor and ripped the package open. He crawled onto the bed while rolling it down his rock-hard dick.

"Please tell me you're ready. I may cry if you're not."

"I'd hate to see you cry." She grasped him, guiding him between her legs.

The tip slipped into her hot, waiting core. Tim growled in ecstasy, pulled away and pushed forward, burying himself to the hilt in one powerful thrust.

Zoe gasped and he stilled, holding his weight above her.

"You okay?" he asked through gritted teeth.

"God, yes." She dug her fingers into his ass and wrapped her legs around his hips. "Fuck me, Tim."

"Gladly."

He dropped to his elbows and used them for leverage as he pulled out and pressed forward again. He set a brutal pace and

Zoe matched him thrust for thrust. He'd imagined being gentle and romantic despite weeks of pent-up desire, but she wouldn't let him.

Her inner muscles clenched around him as if they were unwilling to let him go when he retreated. She dug her nails into his ass in time to his thrusts while she whispered words in his ear that he didn't understand. His balls drew up close to his body and he tried to stave off his orgasm.

That plan went to hell when he felt her bear down on him, followed quickly by rhythmic pulsing around his cock and her shout in his ear.

He shoved a hand under her hips and tilted them, driving as deep as he could go, and shortened his strokes until his orgasm burst from him. He thrust hard into Zoe and matched her shout with one of his own.

One by one his muscles failed him and he lowered all his weight down.

A shudder ran through Zoe's body and she clenched around him again. He groaned and his hips twitched.

"Just a sec and I'll go get a washcloth," he said.

"Not just yet," she whispered. "You feel so good."

He felt her go lax under him and he lifted his head. Brushing the curls away from her face, he whispered her name. Her eyes were closed and her breathing was even. Staring down at her he knew two things—he wanted more and he was a goner.

CHAPTER 18

Zoe cracked open an eye and stared at the mass of curls obscuring her vision. Brushing her hair out of her face, she raised her head and looked around the bedroom. The pillow next to her was still indented from Tim's head. She smiled a Cheshire cat smile and stretched, letting all the aches and twinges remind her exactly how she'd spent the night before.

Wow. Last night had been...wow. She had nothing to compare it to. She'd been demanding and needy and Tim had given her what she wanted and more. He came across so straight-laced and proper. The forceful, sexy man under the starched police uniform was a really nice surprise.

Where was he? Zoe glanced toward the master bath, but the light was off. The alarm clock next to her bed showed a little after eight—did he have to work that morning? She tried to remember whether he'd mentioned it or not, but her brain was still sex-fogged.

She threw on a robe and went downstairs. Her clothes were folded and stacked on the bottom step.

"Tim?"

She found her small purse on the floor next to the entry table and pulled out her phone. The only notifications she had were the nine texts from Elba demanding to know if Tim had given it to her good. Zoe couldn't even fight the smile that tugged at her lips. Hell yeah, he'd given it to her good.

Heading to the kitchen, a small kernel of doubt planted itself in her mind and her smile fell. Why wasn't he there? Why'd he leave without waking her up? Had it been a wham-bam, thank you, ma'am? Was...?

Fuck. She collapsed onto one of the dining room chairs and stared at her to-do list. This was why she hadn't wanted to get involved with anyone. Doubt assailed her. She had no idea what they were doing or what he expected from her. There was no checklist for romance. No linear path she could follow from A to Z and make sure everything was done properly.

A sharp knock at her front door sent hope swirling in her chest. Maybe he'd gone home to take care of some things and had gotten locked out. Trying not to skip to the door, she opened it without checking the peephole.

She should have checked the peephole.

"What are you doing here?" There was no hiding the bitterness and betrayal in her words.

Mark, her no-good, cheating ex-husband, stood on the stoop wearing a hangdog look.

"I haven't seen you in almost a year, Zee. That's how you say hi?"

The corner of her eye twitched. "Shouldn't you be in Florida by now?"

"You wouldn't answer my calls so I decided to stop on the way."

"North Carolina is not on the way from Phoenix to Tampa. How did you even know I was here?"

"I called your mom when you wouldn't answer any of my calls."

She pushed away from the door. "You did what?"

Damn it! She was so tired of her family interfering in her life. Her mother had no right. She was lucky she was still on vacation in the middle of the Caribbean.

"*Why* are you here?"

"I want you back, Zoh." He stepped closer and brushed his hands down her shoulders.

Shrugging him off, she took the added measure of pushing him away from her. "Zoh-ee. Two syllables."

"I thought you liked when I called you Zoh."

"I've never liked it. In fact, I'm pretty sure I told you the first time I met you not to call me that."

He shrugged. "Sorry. It's just a cute name."

"What do you want, Mark?"

"I told you. I want you to come home. I want us to have a second chance."

"You want."

"Well, yeah. I mean, you just left. No email or phone call. You canceled your assignment and got out of the Air Force. That's a little drastic, don't you think?"

She crossed her arms. Slapping her ex-husband across the face probably wasn't a good idea. "Let me get this straight—you sent me divorce papers from Korea with a note that said you'd fallen in love with someone else and she was pregnant. Not only that, but you had your buddies move all your stuff out while I was at work and took your name off the lease, leaving me with an apartment *you* insisted we rent because you needed the extra room and *I* couldn't afford on my own, but I should have informed you of my plans?

"And now you've changed your mind so I should just drop what I'm doing and take you back. Is that about it?"

"Zoe, you love me."

"What's funny about that statement is you didn't say you loved me."

Out of the corner of her eye, she saw Tim approaching across the yard, dressed in gym shorts and a faded Haven Springs Police Department t-shirt. Glancing between him and Mark, there was no comparison. She couldn't even remember what she'd ever seen in Mark to begin with.

Tim pushed passed Mark and kissed Zoe. "Is everything all right?"

"It's perfect," she said.

Tim's gaze searched her face. Satisfied with what he found, he gave her a short nod. "Holler if you need anything."

"I will." She watched over her shoulder as Tim disappeared into the house.

"Who the hell is that?" Mark demanded.

"No one you need to worry about. Goodbye, Mark."

He pushed against the door, as she tried to close it. "Zoe, please! She left me. She's going back to her husband, even though the baby is probably mine."

A small twinge of sympathy hit her. She wasn't a monster. If it had been anyone else, she would have offered a shoulder to cry on, but she couldn't do it with Mark. He was in this mess because of what he'd done—he could deal with it himself.

"I'm sorry for that. I hope you work it out, but it's not my problem."

She closed and locked the door, pressing her forehead it.

"You sure you're okay?" Tim asked from behind her.

"Baby Jesus is punishing me."

"I don't think baby Jesus is punishing you."

Zoe could hear the amusement in his voice. "How do you know?"

Tim pulled her away from the door, turned her and pulled her into a tight hug. "I'm pretty sure that's not how it works."

He rubbed his hands up and down her back and the tension left her body as she relaxed against him.

"Do you want to talk about it?" he asked.

Where to start? With her ex leaving her for another woman or her mother interfering in her life? Impotent anger built in her chest. Her mother.

"What just happened? You got tense again."

"Just a minute." Pulling out of his arms, she stalked to the dining room and picked up her phone from the table and called her mom.

She answered on the second ring. "*Querida*. I'm so glad you called. How are you settling in?"

"Did you tell Mark where I was?"

"Yes. He called and said he wanted to apologize."

"You had no right."

"Don't take that tone with me Zoe Mariana. I'm your mother, I have every right."

"I am not a child. You do not get to make my decisions for me anymore."

"When you abandon a career you've been building for thirteen years just because your marriage hit a snag, yes, I do get to help you make those decisions."

Zoe closed her eyes and clenched her fists. She could barely form thoughts, much less words. "A snag? He cheated on me with a married woman and got her pregnant, Mother."

"All marriages have their challenges."

She could hear the shrug in her mother's voice. Challenges? As if having a cheating husband was the same as working too much or buying a luxury car without discussing it first.

"I am done. Stay out of my life."

"Zoe—"

She pressed the end call button and drew her arm back to throw her phone against the wall, but her wrist was grabbed from behind and the phone pulled from her hand.

"Okay, let's not do any anything drastic."

Tim's calm voice pushed her further toward the edge. "Don't tell me what to do!"

He held up his hands in supplication. "I wouldn't dream of it."

"Quit placating me!"

"Absolutely."

She screamed through clenched teeth and stormed to the kitchen. Slamming cabinets, she jammed a filter into the coffee pot and grabbed the carafe, filling it with water. She was going to regret not being more careful with the grounds, but at the moment she needed something to take her anger out on.

Flipping the coffee pot one, she rounded on Tim. "Where did you go?"

"I had to let the dog out," he said calmly.

"What dog?"

"I'm fostering a dog for Denise's rescue."

"Oh." She didn't have a response for that, but the thought of him fostering a dog dissipated her anger for some reason.

"You ready to talk about it?"

"You're handling me, aren't you? Using your police voodoo tactics to get me to calm down."

His dimples popped out when he grinned. "They don't teach us voodoo at the academy."

"You know what I mean." She took two cups down and pulled the creamer from the fridge.

"I know sometimes it helps to talk about what's making you so angry."

Zoe leaned against the counter, folded her arms, and looked down at her feet.

"Mark got a one-year assignment to Korea. He said it would be good for his career and make it easier for us to get an assignment to Florida since he would be coming off a short tour."

"Did it?"

"Yes. He got a follow-on assignment to Florida and then my assignments manager worked my assignment."

"But you didn't go to Florida." He moved farther into the kitchen and mirrored her position next to her.

The heat from his body permeated through her thin robe and

she leaned against his shoulder. "My assignment notification arrived the same day the divorce papers did."

"You had no idea?"

"None. We'd talked a couple of days before and I had no clue anything was wrong. We even talked about what part of Tampa we wanted to look for a house."

"What an asshole."

She huffed out a laugh. "Yeah."

He shifted and she raised her head from his shoulder. He wrapped his arm around her and tucked her close, resting his chin on her head.

"What did you do?"

"I seven-day opted."

"I don't know what that means."

"When someone gets an assignment notification, they have seven days to either agree to take the assignment or to turn it down."

"And you turned it down. What happens then?"

"I didn't owe the Air Force any more time, so I was out in six months. While I was going through the transition assistance classes, I took the small business track and got the idea for the bookstore. When I was talking to Elba about it, she mentioned the store next to her was for rent and things went really fast from that point."

"Let me get this straight—you got divorced, got out of the military, and started a business all in six months?"

"Yeah." It did sound drastic when he laid it out like that. As if she was some bitter, spurned woman going off the deep end.

His hand grasped the back of her head and he tilted it back to stare down at her. "You're amazing."

"No, I'm not."

"Yes. You are. And I'm glad your husband is an asshole."

She bit back a smile and then remembered he hadn't been there when she'd woken up.

"What?" His eyes searched his face.

"I wondered what had happened when you weren't here when I woke up. I thought you'd left, left."

"Like wham-bam, thank you, ma'am?"

She pressed her lips together when he used the exact words she'd thought. "Something like that."

"Been a while since I've slept next to someone."

"Sorry."

"Don't be. It's my issue. I didn't want to disturb you so I went to let the dog out and feed her."

She nodded. It made sense, but after rehashing everything that had happened with Mark, it was too easy to assume the worst.

"You winced when we cleaned up last night. I wanted to give you a little bit of time to recover."

"Do they teach you mind reading along with voodoo in the police academy?"

"You have very expressive eyes."

Turning her so she was caged against the counter, he guided her head back and pressed his mouth to hers. His tongue traced the seam of her lips and she welcomed him while he invaded her and took possession of her mouth.

Her robe opened and his fingers traced the slit of her pussy. She moaned into his mouth and shifted her weight, parting her legs to allow him easier access. Arousal raced through her like a spark through a firecracker factory.

Tim took full advantage and slowly thrust two fingers into her while his thumb pressed against her clit. "I wanted to wake you up like this, but I wasn't sure if you'd still be sore."

Holy shit, he had magic hands. It was as if his fingers were electrified and sending small shocks through her body. "Not sore."

Hooking her thumbs into the waistband of his shorts, she pulled them down until his erection popped free. She palmed him and ran her hand up and down his length, using her thumb to spread the bead of moisture around the head of his penis.

He thrust into her hand in time to the thrust of his fingers. "I want in you, Zoe. I want to feel you clench around my dick like I can feel you clench around my fingers."

Her muscles spasmed involuntarily and he grinned against her mouth.

"Just like that." He stilled and pressed his forehead against hers. "But I don't have any condoms with me."

She clenched her fist around him. "I have some upstairs."

He grinned at her. "Then we should probably go upstairs."

A small gasp escaped when he lifted her so her legs wrapped around his waist and headed to the stairs.

His dick slid between her thighs and brushed against her clit with each step. She might not even make it upstairs before she came.

Truth be told, she was glad her ex was an asshole too.

CHAPTER 19

B ecause I love books. Who wouldn't want to work in a bookstore?
Zoe smiled at the response written by an applicant for one of the part-time sales associate positions. Who indeed? Wincing at the age of the applicant, only sixteen, she set it in the *maybe* pile.

She'd had a hard time working during high school to earn a little extra money and it had mostly been limited to weekends because of school and studying and sports. She'd still consider it, especially if weekends were as busy as she hoped. Haven Springs didn't have a library and the closest one was twenty minutes away. She planned to have afternoon story time during the week for stay-at-home moms. Maybe she could do something on the weekends as well for those moms that worked.

Damn it. She pulled her planner over and jotted down a note to herself. Her list was getting longer and longer every day.

The doorbell rang and she glanced at her watch, then rubbed her eyes. She was almost cross-eyed from sifting through dozens of applications all while trying to decipher some really bad handwriting. On the one hand, a lot of applications was a good thing.

On the other, it made deciding on the best ones difficult. There were several good potentials for assistant manager.

Pushing away from the table, the doorbell rang again.

"I'm coming," she called out.

This time, she checked the peephole.

"What the hell?"

She unlocked the bolt and opened the door. "What are you doing here?"

"Did you hang up on *Mamãe*?" her brother demanded.

Zoe blew out a sharp breath through her nose. Of course her brother had driven almost three hours to yell at her.

"Stay out of this, João."

"I will not stay out of this. You were disrespectful to *Mamãe*." He pointed a finger at her to emphasize his point.

"She was disrespectful to me."

"You behaved like a child."

That was enough. From him, from her mother, from everyone. She was done letting other people think they knew what was best for her. She might make a few mistakes along the way but damn it, they were her mistakes to make.

"How did I behave like a child, João? Enlighten me. Was it when I told my mother not to tell my cheating ex how to find me?"

She planted her hands on her hips and advanced on her brother. He might have almost a foot of height on her, but her anger was bigger than his.

"Or maybe it was when I decided to finally do something for myself. Or maybe it was when I decided I didn't want to be married to someone who thought so little of me he not only cheated, but got another woman pregnant after telling me for years he wasn't ready for a child."

Zoe took another step forward, not giving João a chance to talk. "I'm not Alicia. I'm not willing to turn a blind eye and look the other way while her husband continuously chooses someone else over his family."

João flinched as if she had struck him. "What does Alicia have to do with this?"

"Seriously? You think I don't know about the girl in Charleston? You think Alicia doesn't know? Maybe the reason you're so willing to defend Mark and what he did is because you're doing the exact same thing to Alicia.

"The only thing I'm grateful for is that Mark did keep putting off having kids so they weren't dragged through this mess. Take care of your own family before you worry about what I'm doing and stay out of my life."

She pivoted sharply and strode back into the house, slamming the door violently behind her. Stalking into the dining room, she paced from one end to the other.

She wished she was a runner. She wished she was one of those people that could tie on a pair of running shoes and run and run until exhaustion replaced the anger.

Really, she wanted to hit something. Someone. Mark or her brother—at the moment, both would make equally satisfying targets.

Agitated energy coursed through her veins with no outlet. She shook her hands and flex her fingers. She was too keyed up to sit back down and continue sifting through applications.

Cursing her brother and her no-good ex under her breath, she stalked back into the foyer and snatched up her keys and purse from the table. Since she couldn't calm down, she'd drive to the store and start unpacking the boxes of books that had been delivered the day prior. As exciting as it was to see actual books in her store, the thought of unpacking and sorting them all had been daunting and she'd planned to leave it until she had hired a few people. Now it seemed like just the thing she needed to get rid of all this excess energy.

Pulling the door opened, she stepped back in surprise. "Mrs.... Mrs. Wilson. Uh...can I...can I help you with something?"

Mrs. Wilson lowered the hand that had been poised to knock and folded them primly in front of her. "Zoe. It's lovely to see you. May I come in?"

Trying to suppress her "what the fuck" expression, Zoe stepped back and opened the door. "Sure." *Que porra e essa?*

Closing the door, she stood awkwardly for a moment before setting her keys and purse down.

Mrs. Wilson looked at the keys on the table. "You were leaving. I can come back another time."

"No. Well, yes, but I wasn't going anywhere specific. I was just going to drive around and clear my head."

"If you're sure..."

"Of course." She led the way into the house. Why wasn't she making excuses to get out of a conversation with Old Lady Wilson?

"Can I get you something to drink? Water or tea?" she asked over her shoulder.

"Tea, please."

"Hot or iced?"

"Iced. It's still unbearably humid outside. I'll be happy when it cools off."

Zoe made a noncommittal sound and fixed two glasses of tea. Setting one on the counter, she took a sip and stared warily through her lashes. Mrs. Wilson didn't look as old as she remembered her. She tried to do the math in her head and realized she probably wasn't all that much older than her own mother. When Zoe was growing up, Mrs. Wilson had always seemed ancient.

"I was watering my flowers and I saw the argument you just had. That was João, wasn't it?"

"Yes."

Mrs. Wilson sipped her tea and set the glass on the counter. "Still as hot-headed as ever, I see."

"Mrs. Wilson, why…?" Zoe cleared her throat. "I'm not trying to be rude, but why did you come over?"

"I wanted to make sure you were all right. I couldn't make out the conversation from across the street, but you looked very upset."

"Oh." The inside of her nose stung and the backs of her eyes watered. Why the hell was she tearing up? And over Old Lady Wilson, of all people, asking her if she was okay. No one had asked if she was okay in a very long time. Not really. They asked if she was sure she'd made the right decision, if she was sure if the divorce and getting out of the Air Force and starting her own business was really what she wanted to do, but no one had asked her if she was okay. Now two people had asked her in one day.

"Thank you. I didn't think you liked me very much."

"Why ever would you think I don't like you?"

If the look on her face was any indication, she was truly bewildered.

"Well, because you always ratted me out to my mom and dad when we were growing up."

"Of course I ratted you out—you were fifteen years old. You had no business sneaking out of your house to gallivant around with your sister. I didn't want you to get in even more trouble you'd regret for the rest of your life."

All Zoe could do was blink at her. "I was sneaking out with Gabby to keep her out of trouble."

"Neither of you should have been sneaking out."

Looking back at her fifteen-year-old self from the eyes of her thirty-two-year-old self, she realized how stupid she had been. Even with the excuse of trying to keep Gabby from doing something monumentally stupid, it had been a bad idea.

"I was like you, when I was younger," Mrs. Wilson said. "Well, I was probably more like Gabby, to be honest. I had an older boyfriend, one my parents didn't approve of. But I was in love and

I ignored them, thinking I knew everything. I got pregnant and I got dumped."

"I'm sorry. I didn't know."

"I wouldn't expect you to. I gave the baby up for adoption, but I've spent my entire life regretting how foolhardy I was. I know I might have seemed very mean to a young girl, but I truly did have your best interests at heart."

"Well. Thank you, I guess, for looking out for us. Even if we did spend most of high school grounded."

"You're welcome. I think it did you a world of good. You grew into a lovely young woman." Mrs. Wilson patted her hand. "Although I was angry when you shaved Buttface."

"Who?"

"Buttface. My cat."

"You named your cat Buttface?" How had she never known that? That information had to be kept from Elba. She'd *never* let Zoe live down shaving a cat named Buttface.

"Its name was Pebbles, but my youngest son always called it Buttface because it looked like someone smushed his nose and the name stuck."

"It was dying of heat exhaustion."

"He was an indoor cat. If you had brought him home, he would have been fine."

"I didn't know that."

"Hmm."

She could hear Mrs. Wilson's thoughts in that "hmm." If Zoe had taken the cat home, she'd have known.

"Tim told me you're opening a bookstore. What's it called?"

Zoe smiled. Tim was talking about her to people. Well, he was talking about her to Mrs. Wilson and while it made sense to talk about one neighbor to another, he was still talking about her to people. "It's called Book Haven."

"I like it." Mrs. Wilson nodded approvingly. "I like the reference to Haven Springs and the fact that books can be a haven for people. Well done."

Damn it. Did she leave an onion out? Her nose was stinging again. A swell of pride bloomed in her chest. Elba and her small business mentor were the only ones who'd offered an encouraging word to her about her bookstore. It felt…good…to have someone commend her for her work.

"When do you open?"

Zoe took a deep breath and glanced at the calendar tacked next to her to-do list on the wall in the dining room. "Six weeks."

Mrs. Wilson followed Zoe's gaze. "Is that your timeline?"

"And one of my to-do lists."

She glanced back at Zoe. "How many do you have?"

"A few," she hedged.

"What are you working on right now?"

"I'm sifting through applications for assistant manager and booksellers."

"Would you like some help? I worked HR for close to thirty years. I've been retired for several, but I can probably help you weed out the riffraff."

Zoe's shoulders relaxed as if someone had come along and lifted a weight off them. "I would love some help."

"Perfect. While we're doing that, you can tell me all about how long you and Tim have been sleeping together."

Know what else made her nose sting? Snorting iced tea through it.

CHAPTER 20

"Hotel Sierra-four, respond to a five-nine-four at four-ten Ellis Street. Caller says to pull around to service alley."

Tim glanced at Kevin and nodded at the radio. Kevin picked up the handset and responded that they were en route. Why did that address sound so familiar? As soon as he turned left onto Ellis Street, he knew—Zoe's bookstore was four-twelve.

Easing down the side street that took him to the service entrance, he saw Zoe, Elba, and a put-out looking man standing close to the back of the building in the alleyway. As soon as he cleared the car door his gaze sought out Zoe. From the set of her mouth, she was stressed but otherwise didn't seem upset. He swore his heart had skipped a beat when he'd realized the address given was right next door to her, even though the call was only for vandalism.

"Finally!" The man broke off from the group and strode over to them. He waved an arm toward the building. "Look at this! Look what they did."

Tim glanced at the building. Someone had spray-painted racial and derogatory slurs down the length of the building between the two service roads. Most of the graffiti appeared to be concentrated on the bookstore and Cafe.

"George, calm down. No one was killed," Elba said. "This isn't an actual emergency. The only reason we even called the cops is to get a report for the insurance."

"It's not the point. I pay my taxes and when I call the police I expect them to arrive in a timely manner."

Ah. He was one of those. "Sir, is one of these businesses yours?" Tim asked.

"They're all mine." He swept an arm out. "I own all these."

"He owns the building, but he doesn't do anything except gouge us on the rent."

Tim pretended he was jotting down a note to hide his smile. He could hear Elba roll her eyes. Glancing at Zoe didn't help—she had pulled her lips between her teeth to keep from doing the same thing.

George spun around. "I do not gouge! I charge a very fair rate based on the location of the building and proximity to the market. Good luck finding better rates than this in this area!"

"Sir," Tim said. "Can you give me a rundown of how you discovered the graffiti?"

"I found it, actually," Zoe said. "I was putting boxes in the recycle bin and I saw the graffiti when I turned to go back inside. I went into the Cafe and told Elba and she called George, then we called you. Well…you know…the police."

His lips quirked when she waved generally in his direction, a slight blush on her cheeks. The memory of her in his bed—asleep on her stomach, clutching a pillow to her with one leg hitched up—flashed through his mind and the blood flow in his body immediately diverted south. Kevin should probably interview her for the report.

"Kevin, why don't you take Zoe's statement? I'll take Elba's and then we can take Mr.…?" He raised his eyebrows at George.

"Baker. George Baker."

"Mr. Baker and then we'll talk to the other store managers."

"Elba?" He cocked his and had her follow him away from Zoe while Kevin pulled her off to the other side.

"Why aren't you taking Zoe's statement?" she asked.

He cleared his throat. *Because all I can think about his bending her over the hood of the cruiser while I show her my night-stick.* Holy fucking cliché.

"I'm sure you know we're…uh…exploring something personal. It wouldn't be professional for me to ask her questions in an official capacity."

"It's graffiti, not a murder scene."

"Yes, but I don't want there to be any perception of impropriety. If the insurance company tries to fight the claim, me questioning my girlfriend might be looked at strangely."

Elba clasped her hands behind her back and swayed from side to side. "You called her your girlfriend."

He counted to three, waiting for her to break out into the *K-I-S-S-I-N-G* song. She just grinned up at him.

"Can we get back to the graffiti?"

Her grin somehow got bigger, but she stopped swaying. "Sure. Like Zoe said, she came in and told me about it."

"You didn't notice it when you arrived this morning?"

"No, it was still dark when I got here."

"You couldn't see it under the light?"

She pursed her lips and scowled. "No. Because the damn light's been out for three months and George is too damn cheap to replace it. I can't replace it myself, because I don't have a fifteen-foot ladder."

He looked up at the light. Sure enough, the bulb was broken. He stepped closer to the other door and saw that light was busted as well.

"And it wasn't there the day before?"

She shook her head. "No. Just the usual dirt and grime."

"What about the security footage?" He pointed at one of the security cameras mounted at the end of the alley.

She braced her hands on her hips. "I highly doubt they work. If you manage to get a recording of whoever did this last night, I'll give you free pastries for the rest of the month."

As good as that sounded, he didn't hold out hope that someone who wouldn't foot the bill to replace a light bulb had working security cameras.

"Thanks, Elba."

"Sure thing. Come inside when you're done and I'll get you guys some coffee to go."

Tim walked over to the building owner, who was kicking at glass on the ground.

"Damn delinquents," he muttered.

"Mr. Baker? I noticed the video cameras at the ends of the alleyway. Do they work?"

"Psh. They're for show. Do you know how much twenty-four-hour coverage costs? More money than it's worth." He had a small, light brown stain halfway down his shirt where coffee seemed to have dripped onto his paunch.

"Right." Tim jotted a couple of notes down to jog his memory later for the report. "So you don't have anything to add for the report?"

"No. I just need the report so I can file the insurance claim so I don't have to pay for this mess."

Tim pulled out a business card. "The number to call for the report is on the back. It'll take seven to ten business days for it to be ready for you to pick up."

"Seven to—! That's ridiculous! How long does it take to type up a report that says 'the building got graffitied?'"

"Right now? Closer to ten business days." Tim held out the business card and stared down at the man blustering in front on him.

George snatched the business card from Tim and stormed down the alley, muttering to himself.

"Ten days exactly," he said under his breath. He clicked his pen, slid it into the loop on the side of his notepad, and joined Kevin and Zoe.

"You good?"

"Yes," Kevin said. "Not a whole lot of information. Just the graffiti." He glanced between them. "I'm gonna go...that way." He pointed down the alley and left them.

"Morning," Tim said.

"Morning." Zoe's gaze trailed down his body. It caused a physical reaction. He could almost feel the brush of her fingertips, leaving behind a trail of goosebumps on his flesh.

"Stop looking at me like that, Zoe."

"Like what?" Her wide, doe-eyes weren't fooling him with her pretend innocence. She knew exactly what she did to him. "You look really good in uniform."

"Should I keep it on tonight?"

He heard her breath catch in the back of her throat. They were absolutely going to have to explore that scenario.

"I'll call you when I get home," he said.

"Okay."

He winked. "You going back in the bookstore?"

"I'm going to grab a cup of coffee from Elba first."

"Be safe today," he said.

"It's just kids being assholes."

"Still. You can't be too careful. Especially now that I know those cameras don't work," he said.

"All right. I'll be careful."

"Thank you."

She stared up at him expectantly and he lowered his head and brushed his lips against hers.

"Is that what you're waiting for?"

"Um…actually, I need you to step back so I can go to the Cafe. But the kiss was nice too." She patted him on the chest.

He took two steps back, clearing a path for her to walk past him. "Yeah."

Laughing, she patted him again and disappeared into the Cafe with a wave over her shoulder.

All he could do was shake his head. He was gone. Head over heels and he had no idea what to do about it. Or whether he even wanted to do something about it. Did he pursue this thing with her? Did she want him to? What about their houses? Who gave up theirs to move in with the other?

Whoa. Whoa.

It was way too early to be thinking about moving in together. They'd only been together for a couple of weeks. It was entirely too soon to be thinking permanent.

Who was he kidding? He'd move in with Zoe in a heartbeat if he thought she'd let him. Hell, Jase had gotten Bree to move in with on the second day they'd met. So what if he'd kind of coerced her into doing it? Tim wasn't going to coerce Zoe. He'd just mention that if she had some stuff at his place, and vice versa, it'd make it easier to get ready in the morning without having to cross the lawn between their houses. It was common sense.

Kevin stood in the middle of the alley looking at the slurs painted on the wall.

"What are you thinking?" Tim asked.

"Zoe said she didn't notice any graffiti yesterday."

"Elba said the same thing. Why?"

"It looks like this was done by two people."

"Why do you say that?"

"'Bitch,' 'whore,' and 'slut' are all in one color and have similar spray patterns, but…the racial slurs are all in another color and have a different spray pattern."

Tim's eyebrows pinched together and he stared at Kevin.

"What? I was into street art for a few years in high school."

"Street art?"

"Yeah. Big colorful murals painted entirely in spray paint. Street art."

"Pretty sure that's still called graffiti."

"Not always."

"Okay, two people spraying graffiti. Since the cameras don't work we can't confirm that or get any footage to positively ID who did it. So other than making note of that in the report in the hopes they do it again, somewhere that has working cameras, there's not a lot we can do about it."

Kevin sighed. "Yeah. I suppose so."

Tim clapped him on the shoulder. "Come on. Let's grab a cup of coffee before we get back on the road. My treat."

"Didn't Elba say she would give us a cup?"

"Yes, but I'm ordering it so it's technically my treat."

"Sure...."

CHAPTER 21

Z oe pushed out of the Cafe and checked the time on her phone. She had about fifteen minutes until the company she'd contracted with arrived to install the point of sale system.

"Zoe." Kevin hung out of the passenger side window of the police car as it idled behind the cars parked in front of the store. "My mom told me to ask you if she can get your number. She'd like to invite you over for dinner."

Stepping off the curb, she sidled between a four-door sedan and a boxy SUV. "Sure. It's—"

"Here." He thrust his phone at her. "You can text it to her."

Trading her coffee for his phone, she spoke as she typed. "Hey Mrs. Moore. This is Zoe. Here's my number:" She finished typing and handed Kevin's phone back to him, taking her coffee. "Thank you."

"See you later," he said.

Tim leaned over so he could see Zoe from the driver's seat. "Bye, Zoe."

She bent at the waist and placed her hand on Kevin's arm, still resting on the window, for balance. "Bye, Tim."

He winked and she stood, waving as they drove off.

Giddy.

She'd never understood what people meant when they said something made them "giddy," but that was the only word she could think of that described how Tim made her feel. Other than sexy and horny. She was excited to see him, to see his name on her phone when he called or texted. Even something as simple as his teasing smile when he said goodbye.

The alarm went off on her phone, reminding her she had an appointment. Shimmying back between the cars, she unlocked the front door of the bookstore. She set her coffee on the checkout counter, then pulled out the placards she'd commissioned for the different book genres, sorting them by where they would be in the store. Fiction—front and center. Non-fiction—stuck in the back along the wall.

She'd special order books if someone was looking for something particular, but she wasn't going to pretend her store was anything other than what it was—a place to escape into a story.

"Excuse me."

She looked up at the woman standing in the door. "Hi. Are you here to install the point of sale system?" She didn't look like an IT person, but who was Zoe to judge.

"Uh, no." She stepped farther into the store. Now that the sunlight wasn't shining behind her like a halo, Zoe knew her initial judgment was correct. This was not a girl who crawled around on the floor running computer cable.

"Do you work here?" she asked.

"I'm the owner. Would you like to submit an application?"

The girl scoffed. "Hardly. I'm here to tell you to stay away from my man." Her tone turned hard and nasty.

"Excuse me?" Who was she talking about?

"I saw you together and I'm here to tell you to back off."

"I think you should leave," Zoe said.

The girl stared Zoe up and down with a derisive glare, crossed her arms, and cocked a hip. "You really think he's going to want you for very long when he can have me? Seriously? You're ten pounds away from being fat. And it doesn't matter if older women are supposed to be more sexually mature, I can rock his world in ways you can't even imagine. And let me tell you, I know just how to put those handcuffs to good use."

"Leave. Now."

She scoffed again and flipped her long, straight hair over her shoulder. "Just remember I tried to warn you when he kicks you to the curb." She sauntered out of the store, slipping on a pair of big sunglasses as she left.

Zoe was going to be sick. She turned away from the door, the latte she'd enjoyed only ten minutes before swirling in a bitter mass in her stomach.

"Don't assume the worst," she whispered.

What else could she assume? Really, she should be thankful. Better to find out now that Tim was cheating on her than later when she was so much more involved. Or was *she* the other woman this time? Was Tim cheating on the young, blond glamazon with her?

She couldn't do this again. She couldn't go through the pain and the hurt because some jerk couldn't keep it in his pants. And he'd stood there and comforted her while she unloaded about what an asshole Mark had been. He'd even agreed with her.

Believing he was the kind of guy who'd lie to her stung. It hurt in a way finding out about Mark hadn't. Her chin quivered and she sucked in a deep breath. She refused to cry over another guy.

"Zoe Acevedo?"

Swiping a finger across her cheek, she plastered on a smile and turned. "Yes."

A tall man stepped through the door, followed by a shorter, younger man. "We're here to set up the point of sale system."

"Great! Where would you like to start?" She had a business to get running. There was no room for mistakes or distractions and she needed to remember that.

"Knock, knock." Tim rapped on the screen door leading into Jase and Bree's kitchen.

"We're in the living room," Bree called out.

He pulled open the door and wound his way through the kitchen. The changes in the house were exponential. Before Bree moved in, it had been the definition of a bachelor's place. Now the small touches Bree had added, as well as the newer furniture, made it feel like a home and not someplace he'd always worried he'd find his brother's body.

Both Bree and Jase stared at him over the back of the large sectional. Charlie, one of Bree's rescue dogs, hopped over to him on his three legs.

Tim reached down to scratch him behind the ears. "Hey, tripod."

"What's up, man?" Jase asked.

"Do you have a few minutes?" Tim asked.

He caught Bree's glance between the two of them. "I'm going to run to the store. You need anything?"

He shoved his hands in his pockets, grateful she was giving him some time to talk alone with Jase. "I'm good, thanks."

Bree patted him on the arm as she walked passed. Jase pushed up from the couch to walk her out and returned with two long-necks, holding one out to Tim.

"Thanks."

Jase pointed his bottle at the back door and led the way out onto the deck. "What's up? You look like someone kicked your dog."

"How did you know Bree was it for you?"

"Huh." He took a drink of his beer and leaned against the railing.

Tim sprawled onto one of the chairs. "*Huh* what?"

He shook his head. "Later. How did I know Bree was the one?"

His gaze became unfocused and he grinned. "When she punched me in the junk."

"Huh." Well, wasn't that some shit. He was pretty sure that was the exact moment he fell for Zoe.

"Huh what?" Jase's eyebrows rose. "Oh shit, did some chick punch you in the junk?"

"Kneed me—on accident. And not some chick—Zoe, my neighbor."

"The one from lunch?"

"Yeah."

"So what's the deal? Is she dating someone? Married? Lesbian? What's holding you back?"

"No. No. No. I don't know. Everything was fine up until last night. I spent the night before at her house, saw her in the morning, then nothing. She was supposed to come over after I got home from work, but she didn't answer her phone or her door when I went over. If I hadn't seen her moving around in her bedroom, I would have been worried that something had happened, but she was fine. She was ignoring me."

"How did you see her in her bedroom?"

"Our rooms face each other. She doesn't always close her curtains."

Jase cocked an eyebrow at him.

"I don't peep. Freak." He didn't share about the first night he'd realized Zoe didn't always close her curtains.

"What did you do wrong?"

"Nothing."

"We always do something. Even when we don't know we did something, we did something."

"Fuck if I know then. When I left her at her store, we were fine."

"Then you need to find out what you did and fix it."

"How do you propose I do that when she won't answer my calls or her door?"

"Figure out a way to see her when she can't escape." Jase pointed his beer at him. "I'm not advocating kidnapping or anything else nefarious, by the way."

"Well, shit. Guess I'll cross that off my list. Thanks for letting me know kidnapping was a bad idea."

"Smart ass. Why're you asking me anyway?"

Tim crossed one of his legs over the other. "Because you seem to have gotten your shit together with Bree and are doing a pretty good job of not fucking it up. Figured you'd have some sage advice to give me."

Jase smirked. "Bree's the first one to tell me when I'm about to fuck up. Why're you really asking me?"

"You never liked Monica."

"Jesus. That bitch."

"That right there." Tim pointed his beer at his brother. "I figured you'd tell me if I should cut my losses if you didn't like Zoe."

"I liked her. A little too shy for my tastes, but I can see the two of you together. The question is, how do you feel about her?"

"I like her. I like her a lot. It's only been a couple of weeks, but last night I felt like a part of me was missing without her there."

Who was he kidding? It was more than like. Not as much as love, but he could see it getting there. Something about Zoe called to him—demanding he keep the worst of the world away from her. She wasn't the kind of woman that needed him to fight her battles for her, but he was more than willing to stand by her while she did.

Jase leaned forward and clinked his bottle against Tim's. "Then figure out how to get your girl to tell you what you did wrong."

CHAPTER 22

Tim parked in the alley behind the bookstore and paused at the service entrance for a moment, wondering if this was the way to handle this. Maybe he should go in the front and give her a chance to tell him to leave. Except that wasn't what he wanted. He had no doubt she'd tell him to leave, but hopefully if he caught her by surprise, with her defenses down, she'd give him an honest answer instead of the bullshit text she'd finally sent him.

The doorknob turned easily in his hand. He was going to have to talk to her about safety—after he got her to talk to him about what was wrong.

He entered the stockroom, crowded with stacks of boxes. Was she planning on shelving all these books herself or had she already hired someone to help her? It had only been two days since they'd really talked and he already felt like he was completely out of the loop of what was happening in her life.

He pushed through the swinging door into the main floor of the bookstore. Wow. His parents had taken them to England one summer and they'd toured a few castles. Zoe's bookstore reminded him of the library they'd seen in one. Instead of harsh fluorescent overhead lighting, she'd installed rustic-looking chandeliers throughout the space. Matching lights on the walls kept the space from being gloomy while still making the space feel like he had walked into someone's house instead of a bookstore. The high backed, overstuffed chair in a side alcove made him want to sit down and pick up a book…and he wasn't much of a reader.

Tim wandered through the empty bookcases until he reached the front of the store. Zoe stood at a high desk with her back to him.

"Zoe."

She jumped and spun, holding a hand to her chest. "*Puta merda!* What are you doing here?"

"You wouldn't answer my calls or texts. I wanted to make sure you're okay."

"I told you I was fine. I'm just busy." She turned back around and continued working on whatever it was in front of her. "So you can go."

He stepped closer to the desk. "You're not any busier today than you were two days ago, Zoe. What happened?"

"I think you should ask your girlfriend that."

"I thought I was," he said softly.

Zoe's head snapped up and she glared at him. Finally, a response. Even if it was anger, he'd take that over the flat, dead voice she had been speaking to him with.

"Then ask your other girlfriend. The one that came into my store and warned me to stop seeing you."

What the fuck? "Zoe, I don't have another girlfriend. You are the only woman I am even remotely interested in."

She left the desk and brushed passed him. "I don't have time for this. Please leave."

"You don't have time for this or you don't have time for me?"

Zoe spun sharply and faced him. Fuck. Tears spilled over her bottom lashes and tracked down her cheeks. The sight gutted him. He never wanted to be part of whatever was causing her to cry.

"I don't have time to feel this way." She pointed at the center of her chest. "I don't have time to be hurt. I don't have time to be with someone who would cheat, whether it's with me or on me."

"I am not cheating—with you or on you. I do not know who this woman is or why she warned you to stay away from me. I swear to you."

Anguish filled her eyes. "I want to believe you. I do. But I don't know how to trust what you're telling me."

Tim stepped closer until he was close enough to reach out and touch her. So when the time was right, he could gather her in his arms.

"Then trust this: I will never cheat on you because my wife cheated on me. Then she left me for her abusive, drug-dealing ex-boyfriend. I will never treat you that way, Zoe. Ever."

She covered her face with her hands and her shoulders shook with her sobs.

"Zoe."

"I don't know what to do." Her voice was muffled behind her hands.

Gently, he wrapped his arms around her until she switched her hands for his chest.

"I'm sorry," she cried.

"Shhh." He pressed his lips to the top of her head. "Don't. It'll be okay. We'll figure this out."

Bending down, he picked her up and carried her back the way he'd come to the chair he'd passed on the way in. It was the perfect size for him to sit and cradle her close while she cried out her anger and fear. He hadn't been lying—they'd figure this out and then he'd pay a visit to whoever had been filling her head with their bullshit.

~

IT TOOK Zoe a good fifteen minutes to stop crying. Sitting in Tim's lap with her head tucked into the crook of his neck while he rubbed her back and whispered nonsense words felt better than it should.

Her chest ached. From her ribs heaving as she cried or from the pain of her heart slowly breaking over the past two days, she didn't know.

"I should have talked to you," she said. "But I was so hurt at the thought of someone doing that to me again, I didn't want to even look at you."

Tim's lips brushed against her forehead again. "Please promise me, if you ever have any doubts, you'll ask me first. I will always be honest with you, Zoe."

She nodded against his neck. "Will you tell me about your ex-wife?"

His chest rose and fell under her as he took a deep breath and released it. "I met Monica while on duty. Her boyfriend had been beating on her and her neighbors called the cops. I tried to get her to press charges, but she refused. It happened a couple more times until I was able to finally convince her to go to a shelter and charge her boyfriend with battery. Turns out he was dealing drugs as well so he got a six-month sentence for possession with intent.

"I was worried about her, so I checked up on her a few times. Checking up on her led to taking her to coffee, then dinner, and a year later we were married. She was always a little skittish...a little secretive, but I attributed it to her history. I tried to get her to see a therapist, but she refused. Said she was fine and there was nothing to talk about."

He paused and she waited, afraid to look at him and see the depth of his pain from being betrayed by the woman he had loved.

"About six months in, I came home one afternoon and she'd packed up all her clothes. She told me she couldn't do it anymore. She couldn't be married to someone who treated her like she was a porcelain doll. Her ex-boyfriend—the one who'd been beating

160

on her—picked her up from our house. She'd been cheating on me with him before we ever got married. The bitch of it was, I couldn't figure out why she married me in the first place."

At least Mark had left her for someone relatively normal—if cheating on your husband and then going back to him with another man's baby could be considered normal. Running off with your drug-dealing abusive ex was a whole other level.

She lifted her head. "You've never treated me like I'm porcelain."

He tucked a curl behind her ear. "You've never seemed fragile."

"I'm afraid the bookstore is going to fail," she whispered. It seemed to be the time for deep confessions.

His lips quirked up, showing off his dimple. "I don't think failing is on any of your checklists."

"I'm serious, Tim." She tried to get up from his lap, only to have his hands wrap tighter around her hips and waist.

"So am I, Zoe. You're the most passionate and driven person I've ever met. I have no doubt this bookstore is going to be a success. The question is, why are you afraid it's going to fail?"

She chewed on the end of her thumbnail. "Because then I'd have to admit to my family that I made a mistake and I screwed up."

"Zoe, I'm pretty sure the only way this bookstore is going to fail is if you didn't put any books in it. It's all Bree and Denise can talk about. I've heard more than a few people at the station talking about it. I haven't seen a whole lot of advertising yet, but people are already excited about having a bookstore in town. If—*if*—this bookstore fails, it's not going to be because you made a mistake and screwed up."

She swallowed hard. She couldn't remember the last time anyone had looked at her with such conviction and belief. Tears burned the backs of her eyes again, spilling down the side of her face.

"Hey. What did I say? Why're you crying again?"

"Thank you for believing in me."

He cupped the side of her face, brushing away a tear with his thumb. "I care about you, Zoe. Of course I believe in you."

Zoe pressed her lips to his. He let her set the pace and didn't try to deepen the kiss. As if he was afraid to do so would push her away. But after two days away from him, she wanted to crawl inside him and never leave. Except that sounded creepy, even inside the confines of her own mind.

She wanted to be with him. In her store. In her dream made into reality. Because if everything was going to be too good to be true, it should all be in the same place.

Nipping at his bottom lip until he opened his mouth, she swept her tongue inside to tangle with his. A small growl sounded in the back of his throat and he still didn't make an effort to move his hands. To grab her ass or her breast.

What did a girl have to do to get laid around here?

She straddled him in the chair and ran her hands down his chest. "Tim."

"Yeah?"

"I want you to make love to me."

She felt his grin against her lips. "Yeah?"

"Yeah." Swiveling her hips, she brushed the apex of her thighs against the increasingly hard front of his jeans.

"Here?"

"Yes." She lifted the hem of his t-shirt and pulled it from his body. "Well, maybe not in the chair since customers are going to sit here at some point in the future."

He smirked. "Good call. Floor?"

"The floor's good." She gripped the sides of his face and meshed her lips to his again.

Finally...*finally*...his fingers dug into the outside of her ass and he held her tightly as he took them to the ground. She wrapped her legs high and tight around his waist, refusing to allow any separation between them until absolutely necessary.

He lifted his head slightly and stared down at her, searching her eyes. "You sure you want to christen your bookstore?"

It was her turn to smirk. "Absolutely."

"All right, then." He yanked off her shirt and before she could really process how quickly it happened, Tim had her naked and his pants were down around his knees.

He sank deep in one smooth stroke and groaned into her neck. "Fuck, I missed you."

An electric current raced through her body, followed quickly by a sense of rightness. Damn, she'd wasted two days of this. Thank God, he was so tenacious and hadn't let her go without a fight.

"I missed you too," she whispered.

He pulled out and thrust back in, quickly finding a rhythm that sent her hurtling toward the edge of her orgasm. Running a hand up her thigh, he pulled her leg over his arm and kissed her calf.

"Your legs are gorgeous," he said. "They were the first thing I saw when you were stuck in that window. I remember thinking they weren't as gorgeous as the ass they were attached to."

He bottomed out and rotated his hips, grinding the root of his cock against her clit.

She sucked in a sharp breath as the first hint of her orgasm hit. A tiny spark sending her body a warning. Watching her, Tim repeated the move again and again until that spark lit and exploded deep in her.

Zoe threw her head back and cried out, digging her nails into his shoulders. He dropped his head beside hers and shorted his strokes until he finally thrust deep with a hard, full-body shudder.

Tim kissed her neck and jawline as their breathing returned to normal. He rose up on his elbows, lifting some of the weight from her.

"I think your bookstore is well and truly christened."

"Not quite yet. There's a few more nooks and crannies I think we should explore."

CHAPTER 23

"Who's the second coffee for?" Elba asked.

Zoe peeked up at her best friend through her lashes. "Tim…"

Elba sat down across from her. "Ah, so you guys made up! Did he break up with the other woman?"

Adding cream to her coffee, Zoe said, "He said he's not dating anyone else and he has no idea who the woman was or why she warned me off him."

Elba's raised eyebrow could give The Rock a run for his money. "And you believe him?"

Zoe understood her disbelief. Neither of them had the best track record when it came to men and their lack of fidelity. "I do. I've been lied to and gaslighted enough that I think I would be able to recognize the signs by now. I think—I know—Tim is telling the truth."

"Okay. As long as you're good with where you are. But I'm giving him the third degree when he gets here."

"Already here." Tim bent down and kissed Zoe, then sat next to her, draping his arm across the back of her chair. "What do you want to give me the third degree about?"

"Is it casual day at the office?" Elba asked.

"My weekend is Friday and Saturday," he said. "Is that part of the interrogation?"

"No. I want to know who this twatwaffle is that tried to warn Zoe away."

"Elba." Zoe really didn't like the tone she was using. She'd told her she believed Tim, that should be all she needed.

"What? Was she not a twatwaffle?"

Zoe had to give her that, but she did it rolling her eyes. "She was a twatwaffle."

"Thank you." She shifted her pointed gaze back to Tim. "So who is she?"

"I have no idea." He looked at Zoe. "What did she look like?"

Zoe shrugged. "Mid-twenties, normal, overly tanned, overly highlighted, way too much makeup, blond girl."

"Hell, that's half the chicks that walk in here," Elba said.

Tim tugged on one of Zoe's curls absentmindedly. "I honestly don't know anyone that fits that description. The only blonde I have more than a passing acquaintance with is Denise and you've met her. Plus, she's married so she wouldn't be warning you off me. Unless you hate dogs. Then all bets are off and you're on your own."

Zoe grinned. "I don't hate dogs."

Tim kissed her. It was quick, but he did it in front of Elba without any hesitation. "Then you're good."

"So no idea who this chick is?" Elba asked.

"None. I'm not cheating on her, Elba."

"Hmf."

Zoe sighed and rolled her eyes heavenward. She loved Elba and loved that she was protective of her, but she also wasn't one to let something go.

"I need to check on orders and customers."

"Before you go, did you decide on where you wanted the

cameras? The security guy will be here at two to install the system."

Elba shrugged. "One in the kitchen and one in the dining area, I guess. Let him figure out the best positioning." She topped off their coffees and returned the pot to the coffee maker before disappearing into the kitchen.

Tim angled his body toward her. "Do you mind if I hang out with you today?"

"I'll be working in the bookstore all day."

"I'll make a deal with you. Put me to work today so you can spend the day with me tomorrow."

"Tim—"

"One day, Zoe. I know how important this is to you and if you don't get everything done, then I'll be right back here with you to take care of it tomorrow."

She chewed her lip and cataloged everything she wanted to get done today and tomorrow. If Tim helped her, they might be able to get it all knocked out.

"Okay, but if we don't get everything done, the deal's off."

"I can work with that."

If he kept smiling at her like that, they weren't going to get anything done. At all.

"HOW LONG HAVE YOU BEEN AWAKE?"

Zoe tilted her head back and found Tim looking at her through sleepy eyes.

"Not long."

"What are you thinking so hard about?" He ran his fingers through her hair, brushing it over her shoulders.

"Mentally going through my checklist."

"No checklists. You promised to spend the day with me. My plan doesn't involve checklists."

"That's today. Tomorrow is a different story. I need to get ready for next week. I'm only two weeks away from a soft opening. I have employees to train and shelves to stock and all sorts of things to freak out about."

"Why a bookstore? Why not a smoothie bar?"

Zoe snuggled into his shoulder as his fingers traced up and down her back. "A couple of reasons. We always spoke Portuguese at home before my mom married my step-dad. I knew English, but not very well. When we moved to the U.S., I struggled and had to take English as a second language in school.

"They paired us with older students to practice our reading and vocabulary. I was paired with a girl who loved fantasy books —dragons and witches, shapeshifters and faeries. We read those books instead of the boring material they gave us and my love of reading was born.

"My step-dad was in the Army and we moved three more times before we ended up here. Every time in a new school was hard, especially since I wasn't a tall, white girl with blond hair."

Tim rolled over so he was on top of her. "I like that you're not a tall, white girl with blond hair."

She smiled. "Anyway. Books were my escape when I was in that awkward, no-friends stage of getting to a new place."

He peppered soft kisses down her neck and across her shoulders. "What's the other reason?"

"Huh?" His kisses were distracting. Especially when she parted her legs and he settled between them.

"You said there were a couple of reasons. Loving books is one. What's the other one?"

"Oh. Have you heard of The Ripped Bodice?"

His head popped up. "The what?"

She chuckled at the confused look on his face. "It's an independent bookstore out in Los Angeles that sells only romance books. The name is a play on calling romance books 'bodice rippers.'"

"Oh. No. Never heard of it." He resumed trailing kisses down her chest, scooting lower until his mouth was centered between her breasts.

"Not surprising. I was inspired by them. I wanted to open a small bookstore that showcased independent authors." Lifting her shoulder, she tried to direct him closer to her breast without grabbing his head and putting it where she wanted.

Instead, she felt his teasing smile against her skin. Jerk. He knew exactly what he was doing.

"Are all the books in your store going to be romance books?"

"Not all of them. Could you go left or right, please?"

His shoulders shook as he laughed. "Is there somewhere in particular you want me to go?"

Grasping his hair, she tugged on his head. "You know exactly where I want you to go."

"What if I move down instead?"

"That would be good too."

He shifted down lower and she hummed, running her hands over the muscles of his shoulders. She was already hearing bells.

"Someone's at your door," Tim said.

"If you keep going, you'll be right at my door," Zoe said.

He chuckled and kissed just below her bellybutton. "No, sweetie. Your actual door. That was the doorbell."

"Maybe they'll go away."

No such luck—the doorbell rang again. This time she recognized the sound. *"Droga."*

Tim rolled off her and she sat up. "I swear if they aren't selling anything good, I'm going to punch them."

"Maybe don't tell the cop you're planning on committing assault."

"Yeah, well, I can blame it on my raging hormones. Women get off for that kind of stuff all the time."

He curled around her and kissed her hip. "Hurry back and I'll make sure *your* doorbell gets rung."

Zoe pulled on a t-shirt and a pair of shorts and headed downstairs, dragging her hair into a messy bun on the way.

Checking the peephole, she dropped her head against the door and groaned. A salesman would have been preferable. At least that encounter would have been short. She opened the door for her sister-in-law. She'd always been put together whenever Zoe had seen her. Now Alicia's eyes were red and puffy and her face devoid of makeup.

"Alicia. What's wrong? Are the kids okay? João?"

She shook her head and looked down briefly. "They're all right. The kids are anyway."

Zoe's stomach dropped. "Did something happen to João?"

"No. No, he's fine. Physically. It's— Can I come in?"

"Of course. I'm sorry." She stepped aside and let Alicia pass her.

"Do you want something to drink?" She asked over her shoulder as she led her into the living room.

"Is it too early for wine?" Her laugh came out as a half sob.

"I don't think it's ever too early if the occasion calls for it. I have some."

Alicia shook her head and sat on the love seat. "No. Water's fine."

"I'll be right back." She fixed two glasses of water and grabbed a box of tissues from the bathroom on the way back, handing both to Alicia.

"Thank you."

Zoe sat in the chair next to the love seat, curling her legs under her. "What's going on?"

"João came clean. He admitted to the affair." She looked up as if trying to keep the tears from spilling over. "He also told me what you said."

"I'm sorry. I had no business dragging you into our fight."

Alicia looked at her, tears spilling unchecked down her cheek. "You must think I'm so weak."

"What? No. I don't think that at all. I think we're two very different people living two very different lives. I do think my brother is an asshole, though."

She pulled a tissue from the box and wiped under her eyes, bunching the tissue in her fist. "You were right, though. I knew, but I could ignore it as long as I didn't really *know*. I could pretend nothing was wrong as long as neither of us admitted the truth.

"I kept telling myself it didn't matter about the other women because it was me he married and me he came home to. But then I would wonder why I wasn't enough. Why weren't the kids and I enough to keep him happy and what was I teaching my kids if I continued to accept this?"

Zoe moved to the love seat and grasped Alicia's clenched hands in hers. "I don't have any answers for you."

"He blames you."

"That doesn't surprise me."

Alicia met her gaze. "I came by to tell you it's not your fault. I should never have let it go on for so long."

"It's not your fault either, Alicia. João did this to himself."

She shook her head and looked up again. "I should have taken responsibility for me and the kids but…I wanted him to *choose* us. I wanted him to choose *me*."

"I don't think that's too much to ask for." Damn, this felt like her fault. Even though João was the one cheating on his wife, if she hadn't said anything to him, would Alicia be here? "What are you going to do?"

"I don't know. I kicked him out of the house."

"What do you want to happen?"

"I love him." A small sob escaped. "Even with everything he's done, I still love him. I want my family whole, but if he can't choose us…" She took a deep breath and sat up a little bit straighter. "I can't stay with him, even though it will rip a hole in my heart."

"Just so you know—I'm on Team Alicia. If you need anything, let me know."

That earned her a watery smile. "Thank you. No matter what happens I will never keep you from JJ and Mary. You're their favorite."

"Did you drive this whole way here just to talk to me?"

"No. I took the kids to Raleigh for the weekend to see my parents. I told them I was running to the store. I needed a little time away. It was getting hard putting on a happy face for them and pretending everything is okay. I should really head back. Thank you for talking to me."

"There's no need to thank me. You're my family."

Zoe walked her out to her car. Alicia promised to bring JJ and Mary by to see her at the bookstore on their way home the next afternoon and she made a note to put a couple of books aside for the kids.

Once Alicia had turned the corner and was out of sight, Zoe rubbed her hands over her face and sighed. Alicia may not blame her, but it didn't stop her from blaming herself.

She'd lashed out. Being angry at João wasn't a good enough reason for dragging his and Alicia's marriage into the argument. She'd never expected João to confess to Alicia because he didn't see anything wrong with what he was doing. Zoe couldn't help but wonder if he'd done that to prove to her that Alicia wouldn't care either but it'd blown up in his face instead.

Which still made it her fault.

She closed the door softly and leaned back against it. Tim sat halfway up the stairs.

"Eavesdropping?" she asked.

"Absolutely. I'm a cop. Being nosy is part of my job." He walked farther down and sat again a few steps from the bottom, putting them at eye-level. "I came down to make sure you weren't trying to hide the body of a door-to-door salesman."

Her lips quirked up.

"You okay?" he asked.

"Yeah. Sucks though. I love Alicia."

"In case I haven't made it clear—I'm choosing you."

There was no stopping her smile. "Yeah?"

"Yeah. For as long as you'll let me."

CHAPTER 24

"Wow. I didn't realize all this was out here." Zoe gazed out the window of Tim's truck as they passed miles and miles of trees interspersed with open fields.

Tim glanced at her from the driver's seat. "You've never been out this way?"

"I don't think so. I mean, we may have come out this way when I was in high school, but I haven't since I've been back."

"I wanted to ask...why did you come back here instead of opening a bookstore in Arizona?"

"My family is all out here on the east coast. As difficult and trying as they are, I love them. My oldest nephew is twelve and my youngest niece is five. I missed seeing them grow up. Plus, the rent was cheap."

She loved when his dimple popped out. It made him look younger and a little mischievous.

He twirled one of her curls around his finger. "Lucky for me then."

"How far out do Jase and Bree live?"

"They're only about thirty minutes to downtown Raleigh, but

when you get off the highway and away from all the towns, it makes it seems a lot farther."

He slowed and turned onto a hard-packed dirt road.

"How far off the beaten path are they?"

"Not that far. This is the back way to their house. It cuts across their property. You used to have to drive all the way around to get to this part, but Bree made Jase put in a road from the house to the pond so they didn't have to drive around to get to it. It had the added benefit of providing a shortcut to the house."

They rounded a bend in the road and the pond came into view. "Wow. I'd prefer to drive by this every day too." She squinted at the water's edge. "Is that a grave?"

Tim slowed the truck to a stop and put it in park.

"What's wrong," she asked.

He shifted in his seat so he was facing her. "The grave is Jase's best friend. They grew up together and served in the Army together. He took his life a few years ago."

"Oh." She glanced at the headstone.

She'd lost two friends to suicide. They hadn't been really close friends, but their decision had still impacted her deeply.

"Jase took it hard. For a while, my sister, my parents, and I worried that he was going to do the same."

"He got help?"

"He got Bree."

She shook her head. "I don't understand."

"Bree drew him out of his shell. Helped him heal, got him to go to counseling, and helped him get better. Sometimes I can still see the shadows in his eyes, but they're fewer and farther between than they used to be."

"He's lucky he has her," she said quietly. Having the right person in your life made all the difference in the world.

"He is." He threaded his fingers into the nape of her neck. "Just goes to show you—all a good man needs is a great woman."

Her. He was talking about her. She'd never had anyone look

soulfully into her eyes, but that was exactly what Tim was doing. The depth of his emotion poured from his gaze. He brushed his thumb across her cheekbone and lowered his head to hers, kissing her gently.

When he pulled away, she was sure her own eyes were full of cartoon hearts.

"Ready for barbecue?" he asked.

"Definitely."

THE SPANISH INQUISITION had nothing on Bree and Denise. They asked her everything from where her favorite place was growing up to her favorite author to whether Tim had invited her to the wedding because if he hadn't, Bree would make sure she had an invite.

"Oh. I— We—" It was the very definition of awkward.

"Tim," Bree shouted.

"Please don't put him on the spot." What if he said he wasn't inviting her? What if he'd already invited someone else before they started dating.

"It's fine. It's probably one of those guy things where he assumes you're going to do something so he never gets around to asking."

"I hate it when Chris does that," Denise said.

"You hollered?" Tim came in from the back deck, followed by Jase, Chris, and the three dogs.

"You haven't invited Zoe to the wedding yet?" Bree asked.

"Considering I haven't received my invitation, I thought it was a bit presumptuous to invite her to a wedding I'm not even sure I'm attending."

"You're the best man," Denise said. "You're obligated to be at the wedding whether you get an invitation or not."

"I'm the best man?" Tim wasn't being snarky. He seemed to

have no idea he was going to be his brother's best man.

"Are you serious?" Bree asked.

Denise leaned close and whispered, "It's going to get guy sappy in a minute."

"Guy sappy?"

She tilted her head toward the three men. "Watch."

"Jase, you haven't asked Tim to be your best man?" Bree demanded.

"Why would I have to ask him? Of course he's my best man." He looked at Tim. "Who else would I ask?"

Denise nudged Zoe with her elbow. "See? Guy thing."

Tim pointed at Chris. "Your best friend."

"Dude. You're my brother. Of course you're my best man."

"I'm honored."

Jase pulled him into a back-pounding hug. "Can't believe you thought I'd ask someone else. Asshole."

"Shut up."

They released each other with one last pounding and Tim turned to Zoe, his eyes suspiciously bright. "So...want to be my plus one to my brother's wedding?"

Zoe grinned. "When you ask like that, how can I refuse?"

He hugged her and kissed her temple. "Sorry I abandoned you. I hope they weren't too bad."

"It was fine. It shows they care."

"Did they ask you to foster a dog?"

"No. Why?"

He looked down at her with a serious face. "Don't fall for it. Whatever they tell you. It's a trap. They give you a dog and you're never free. Even if they find a home for that dog, there's another dog waiting in the wings. A sweeter dog. A cuter dog. It's a never-ending cycle of dogs."

"But I like dogs."

"Jesus. Don't ever tell them that."

"Don't tell us what?" Bree asked.

"That I like dogs," Zoe said.

Tim threw up his hands. "Oh God. Now you've done it."

Bree smacked him on his stomach with the back of her hand. "Quit it."

"Oh, yeah," Denise said. "That reminds me. We found a possible forever home for Mitzy."

"Is it a retirement home? Because I'm pretty sure that's the only place that will have the same energy level as that dog. If I couldn't see her chest moving, I would have thought she'd died a couple of times."

"Not quite. The person interested is a retiree. It's one of Gran's neighbors," Denise said.

"I hope he isn't interested in getting a dog to increase his activity level."

Tim's phone rang and he pulled it out of his pocket, glancing at the display. "Hey, man, what's up?"

He stepped away from Zoe. "Do you need me to call a cruiser?...I'm about twenty minutes out...I've got Zoe with me...I don't care if you don't want to get her in trouble, you call a cruiser at the first hint she's unhinged...I'll be there as soon as I can."

Thumbing the display, he looked at the group. "We need to go. Kevin's got a situation at his apartment."

"Is he okay?" Zoe asked.

"Yes, but I think I know who the woman is who warned you off."

HE CALLED A CRUISER ANYWAY. After almost losing Bree to a stalker a year ago, he wasn't willing to take any risks, no matter what Kevin said about how Ashley was acting.

"So you think this girl likes Kevin and she thinks we're an item for some reason," Zoe said.

"You'll have to take a look at her to know for sure, but I think so." Tim took the corner faster than was wise, but he wanted to get to Kevin's quickly.

Zoe grasped the handle above the door as she swayed with the motion of the truck. "But why does she think Kevin and I are together?"

"I think she's been following Kevin. He mentioned she joined his gym and she somehow figured out where he lives, so maybe she saw you two together and thought you were interested in him."

They reached Kevin's apartment complex and he wound through the buildings, slowing down only as much as necessary for the speed bumps. He breathed a small sigh of relief when he saw two cruisers double-parked in front of Kevin's apartment.

He parked behind one of the cruisers. "Stay here."

"But—"

"Please, Zoe. You'll be safe in the car."

She sat back in the seat. "Okay. Be careful."

"I will."

He jogged up to the open front door.

"I can't believe you called the cops!"

The girl was trying to pull her arm out of the grasp of one of the officers as she yelled.

"I called in for backup," Tim said as he entered the apartment.

"You called him?" She pointed at Tim, but asked Kevin.

"You wouldn't leave." Judging by Kevin's tone, this had been a theme for a while.

"Of course I'm not leaving, we belong together."

"Ugh." Kevin threaded his hands through his hair. "We do not belong together."

Kevin was obviously too nice to deal with this. Tim didn't have the same problem. "Ashley—it's Ashley, isn't it? Right now you're trespassing. You've been asked to leave a domicile that is not your own and you have refused. If you don't leave of your own volition, right now, you will be taken to the station and charged. If that happens you're looking at jail time and a fine."

One of the other officers cocked an eyebrow at Tim. Yes, he was overplaying the penalty. At most she was probably looking at second-degree trespassing. The penalty was a two hundred dollar fine and twenty days in jail, which usually didn't happen.

"Kevin, please don't do this. I just want to make you happy."

"It's not going to happen."

"If you'll stop seeing that other woman, I know it can."

"What other woman?" Kevin asked.

"The one from the bookstore. I don't know what you see in someone so old. You'd think she'd have gotten the hint after the warnings I gave her and told her to back off."

That confirmed Tim's assumption that Ashley was the one who'd warned Zoe off.

"What warnings?" Tim asked.

"Is she talking about Zoe?" Kevin asked.

"Yeah. She confronted her at the bookstore and told her to stay away from you." He looked back at Ashley. "What warnings?"

"Nothing serious. I spray-painted the back of her store."

"Did you slash her tire?"

She looked away. "No."

She was lying. Tim knew it but didn't have a way to prove it.

"Kevin, I love you." Her voice took on a cajoling tone. "We're perfect for each other."

"Jesus." Kevin turned away and turned back. "I'm gay! There. I said it. I'm not interested in you because I'm gay and I have a boyfriend."

He laced his hands behind his head and stared up at the ceiling.

Tim crossed his arms, smiled, and waited for the explosion in three...two....one.

"You lying bastard. Do you honestly think I'd believe you're gay? I've seen you with that woman hanging all over you," she shouted.

The officers looked at Tim and he nodded. One of them pulled her arms behind her back and she struggled while the other officer snapped the cuffs on her.

"You can't do this." She dug in her feet and tried to pull out of their hold. "Let me go."

"Ma'am, please stop struggling."

"You're going to regret this," she yelled as they dragged her through the open door. "You're both going to regret this."

"Fuck." Kevin threw up his hands and paced into the kitchen.

Tim gave him a level stare when he returned with a beer. "You need to get a restraining order."

"Yeah."

One of the officers returned and jotted down Kevin's contact information. On his way out the door, he paused and turned back. "Do you really have a boyfriend?"

"Yeah. What about it?" Kevin asked.

"Eh." He shrugged. "My brother's single."

CHAPTER 25

Z oe glanced at her watch and shook her wrist when the digital display didn't immediately show. Fifteen minutes. Nine hundred seconds and she would open the doors to her dream.

"*Meu Deus*," she whispered. Why did she ever think this was a good idea? Why did she think she could succeed and do this on her own?

"There you are." Mrs. Wilson turned the corner of the row Zoe was hiding in. "What's wrong?"

"I think I'm having a panic attack. Maybe an anxiety attack. I don't know what the difference is but I know I'm freaking out."

Mrs. Wilson grasped her by the shoulder. "Zoe. It's a soft opening. It's Tuesday so there won't be a lot of shoppers. This gives us time to work out any kinks and bugs before the weekend."

Thank goodness Mrs. Wilson had agreed to fill in as the assistant manager until Zoe found someone permanent. She was the rational, level-headed person Zoe needed right now. "I know, but it's still a big deal. What if no one comes in? What if it's a big, horrible failure?"

"People will come in. You will not fail. Everything is going to be fine. You have a checklist, right?"

"Yes." She nodded. "It's on the checkout desk."

"All right. Then that's all you need." She smiled reassuringly. "Ready?"

Zoe took a deep breath and pictured the checklist in her head. Every item on every list had been checked and double checked. She'd been working non-stop for the past week and a half, often falling into bed too exhausted to do more than cuddle up next to Tim. Rebecca and Seth, her full-time employees, were trained and as excited as she was nervous.

"Yes. I'm ready."

"Then let's go." Mrs. Wilson turned her and gave her a small push toward the front of the store.

Everyone turned when they broke through the bookcases and walked toward the desk.

"I was wondering where you were," Elba said. "I brought coffee for everyone and a platter of mini scones for customers."

"Thank you," Zoe said. She turned to the other two. "Remember to write down anything that goes wrong in the log at the desk so we can address it before the grand opening in two weeks. If they come from the Cafe, they get ten percent off their purchase and Elba and her staff are going to remind their customers when they pay. Same goes for here, if they buy something here, remind them they get a discount at the Cafe."

They all nodded while she spoke. They'd already gone over all this, but it helped her go through it all again.

"Seth, can you put the sandwich board out front and I'll go open the doors to the Cafe."

"I'll go around and unlock them from the other side." Elba pushed away from the counter she'd been leaning on and followed Seth to the front door.

"Thanks."

Zoe walked over to the wall and released the locking mechanisms on the shelves. Seconds later one side swung open when Elba pushed from the other side.

"Ladies and gentlemen, the Book Haven is now open," Elba said, gesturing with a flourish.

"You're a dork," Zoe said.

"But I'm your dork." Elba pulled her into a side hug. "Go sell lots of books."

The next three hours were a blur as a steady stream of customers kept them all busy.

"Zoe, I need your help," Rebecca said.

Zoe approached the back side of the checkout counter where a customer was waiting. "Sure. What do you need?"

"I can't find the author this customer is looking for."

"Who's the author?"

"Amber Finch?"

Zoe frowned. "Why does that sound familiar? You searched the database?"

"Yes, she's not listed."

Zoe looked at the older woman waiting patiently on the other side of the counter. "Do you remember the name of one of the books? Maybe we aren't spelling the author's name correctly."

"The one I read about is Phoebe Moon and the Sneeze Snatcher. It's a middle-grade novel. There's supposed to be a whole series of them. I'd like to get them for my granddaughter, but I haven't been able to find them anywhere."

"Where did you read about them?" Zoe asked.

"In one of Jamie Farrell's novels."

That was an author Zoe was familiar with. "Was it one of her Misfit Bride books?"

"Yes! It's one of my favorites."

"Ah. The Phoebe Moon books aren't real books," Zoe said.

"What do you mean? There are several quotes in the Misfit Bride book. Where would she get the quotes if there aren't any books?"

"They aren't published—Jamie Farrell made them up as part of the Misfit Bride story. The heroine in her book is the author of the Phoebe Moon books, but it's all fiction."

The woman opened and closed her mouth a few times. "Is she going to write any Phoebe Moon books?"

Zoe shook her head. "I really don't know."

"Well! I'm going to write to her and demand she write Phoebe Moon books." She left the counter, muttering to herself about the nerve of some people.

Zoe's shoulders shook and her eyes watered from trying not to laugh out loud.

Rebecca was having the same problem and snorted through her nose before turning away to hide her face.

"Why don't you go get lunch while there's a lull," Zoe said. "Elba said you guys could have an employee discount."

"Thank you. I'll be back in thirty minutes."

"When you get back, tell Seth he can go."

Zoe regretted sending Rebecca to lunch exactly twelve minutes later when three moms came in with seven children, at least three of whom were crying.

"Welcome to the Book Haven." She plastered a smile on her face that felt more like a grimace.

"Will, watch your sister!" one of the moms called after a few of the kids heading to the back. She turned to Zoe. "Hi. Just so you know, you're probably going to get a lot of moms in here in the next few days. One of the local mommy bloggers posted a picture of that tree house and it's making the rounds on social media."

"Oh. That's...that's good," Zoe said. It was good. It was. Maybe if she repeated it to herself enough times, she would believe it. That was exactly why she put the loft in—to attract parents and young readers. Although it would be nice if they didn't all descend on her and the bookstore at the same time.

"Make sure you come back for the grand opening. Ten percent

off the entire store, plus lots of book prizes." Mrs. Wilson handed a flyer to the distracted mom.

"Thanks." She shoved it into her already overstuffed bag without looking at it and followed the sounds of shrieks and screams.

Zoe looked at Mrs. Wilson and saw a grinning Tim approaching from the front entrance. Her day improved exponentially.

"Wow. Look at this place." He bent down and kissed her—right in front of Mrs. Wilson. "I told you you had nothing to worry about."

"Did she say she was worried about people not showing up?" Mrs. Wilson asked.

"Yes, and that it would fail."

"Silly girl." Mrs. Wilson winked at Tim, not even trying to hide it from Zoe.

"You two can quit talking about me like I'm not here," she said.

Mrs. Wilson grinned at her. "I'm going to help Seth at the register."

"All right." She turned to Tim. "What are you doing here?"

He kissed her again, lingering a little longer than before. "I know you were nervous this morning and I wanted to see how you were doing."

"You're checking up on me?"

"Yes."

Pure joy raced through her veins. "Thank you." She stood on her toes and kissed him again.

"Where's Kevin?" she asked.

"Next door, getting us a couple of coffees."

"Really? You're sending the rookie to fetch your coffee for you?"

He smiled at her. "He offered. I think he's interested in something not on the menu."

"What's not on the menu?"

His eyebrows rose and he stared at her expectantly.

What's not on the...? "Oh. Oh! Are he and Rob seeing each other?"

"He hasn't confirmed it, but I think so. He was very eager to get coffee for us."

"Well, yay for them. Rob's a good guy."

"Good to know." He waved at a little boy peeking out from between his mother's legs while she paid for her purchase.

The door opened again and Denise walked in, followed by her large Mastiff mix. It was only the second time Zoe had seen the dog with her service dog vest on.

"Oh my God. This is heaven." She stopped next to Zoe and Tim. "I've always dreamed about having a house with a library like this. It's beautiful, Zoe."

"Thank you so much." She swept her gaze over the store. "It's exactly how I imagined it in my head."

"I'm going to browse." Denise took a step forward, stopped and turned back. "No issue with Sprocket, right?"

"Of course not."

Watching Denise walk away, Sprocket close at her side, gave Zoe an idea.

"I need my planner." She hurried over to the desk and wrote a reminder to look into the reading to rescue animals program she'd seen online while it was fresh in her mind. Finished jotting down her notes, she glanced up to find Tim leaning against the counter, watching her.

She tucked a stray curl behind her ear. "What?"

"I didn't want to interrupt you in the middle of your thought process, but I need to grab Kevin from next door so we can finish our patrol."

She walked around the counter. "Sorry, I got distracted."

"Don't apologize for being you."

The soft, appreciative look on his face spread warmth through her chest.

"I need to go check on the children's area anyway since it was overrun right before you came in."

"Okay. Call me when you leave the store?"

She nodded. A quick peck and he was gone. She sighed, watching him walk out the door. Her insides turned into a gooey mess and it wasn't just from the way his ass filled out his pants. He'd taken time out of his day to check on her. He made sure she'd text him when she left the store.

She'd balked the first time he'd asked her to, but after he'd explained about Bree's attack she understood. Knowing Kevin's crazy stalker might not be over her crazy didn't help.

So she told him. Because he worried and he cared and she liked that he worried and he cared.

A shriek rent the air and she slowly turned to face the back of the store. She shared a wide-eyed look with Mrs. Wilson. Beside her, Seth put his finger on the tip of his nose, the universal sign for "not it." Zoe rolled her eyes and headed to the children's books section. Her store, her headache. Hopefully she wouldn't have to kick anyone out for baby brawling. That would definitely make the mommy blogs and not in a good way.

THE BOOKCASES WERE TOO TALL. Zoe couldn't even reach the fourth shelf and the book she needed was all the way at the top. The shelves weren't supposed to be this high—she didn't have any ladders.

Where was that buzzing coming from? She spun in a circle but couldn't find the source of the noise. Trying to follow the sound, she turned down aisle after aisle with no luck. The sound would go away and then would return coming from the right, but when she looked she couldn't find what was making the noise. Even when she put her ear to the wall.

Where had the shelves gone?

"Zoe, wake up. You're phone's vibrating."

Her eyes snapped open. "There are bees in the bookstore."

"What?" Tim leaned over and turned on the lamp next to his bed.

Zoe flinched away from the light. "I was dreaming about the bookstore. I kept hearing bees but I couldn't figure out where they were and then all the books were gone and it was just a room of walls."

"Well, the bees can be explained by your phone vibrating on the table. It's been going non-stop for the last few minutes." Tim braced himself on his elbow. "I'm no psychologist, but I'd guess dreaming about the books being gone is your mind worrying about not being successful."

"I hate my brain sometimes." Her phone vibrated on the table again and she picked it up. "Elba, it's three in the morning."

"Zoe. I'm so sorry."

She sat up in bed, driven by Elba's anguish pouring through the phone. "What happened? Are you okay? Where's April?"

She threw off the covers and picked up her jeans from the floor before she even finished asking the first question.

"It's the Cafe. And the bookstore." Elba's shaky breath was audible. "There's a fire."

CHAPTER 26

Tim wouldn't let her drive herself there. It was probably a good idea because she didn't remember the ride. Her mind was going a mile a minute, thinking of the worst and hoping that maybe it was only a little smoke damage and all she'd need to do was air out the store. But Elba wouldn't have sounded the way she had on the phone if it was only a little smoke damage.

The fire department had the roads blocked at each end of the street. The only reason they were able to get around the barricades was because Tim flashed his badge and walked them in. Even then, they were stopped on the other side of the parking lot across from the stores.

Zoe pressed her hands over her mouth. The entire street was painted in an eerie orange glow and all four stores were engulfed in flames. The worst of the fire seemed to be concentrated on the cafe and the salon.

The tears in her eyes had nothing to do with the black, acrid smoke filling the air.

"Stay here," Tim said. "I'm going to go see if I can find out anything. Okay?"

She nodded. Where else was she going to go?

Her phone buzzed in her pocket and she swiped to answer it.

"Where are you?" Elba asked.

Zoe had to press a finger to her opposite ear to hear Elba over the roar of the fire and water. "I'm on the other side of the parking lot. Tim went to see if he can find out anything."

"I'll be right there," Elba said.

It could have been hours or it could have been seconds later when Elba wrapped her arms around her.

"I'm so sorry," her friend whispered.

Zoe squeezed her eyes closed. Maybe it was all a dream. She was still stuck in the dream with the bees and it had morphed into a nightmare driven by her worst fears. Except she could hear the crackle of the fire and feel the heat on her face.

"What happened?"

Elba's hair brushed Zoe's cheek as she shook her head. "I don't know. I got the call from the alarm company."

Damn it, she hadn't checked for any other missed calls after she answered Elba's.

"Hey." Tim returned and Zoe wiped her eyes and released Elba, but kept an arm around her waist.

"What did they say?" she asked.

"I talked to the on-scene commander. They're working to keep it contained to your building and not let it jump to the adjacent buildings, but the chemicals in the hair salon are making it difficult to put out the fire."

Zoe closed her eyes again and took a shaking breath.

"Do they know how it started?" Elba asked.

"They won't know until they get the fire out and the investigator can go in, but…."

"But what?" Zoe asked.

Tim braced one hand on his hip and ran the other hand through his hair. "Based on how the fire spread, they think it started in either the salon or…the Cafe."

"It wasn't the Cafe." Elba shook her head frantically and faced

Zoe. "It can't have been. We have a freaking checklist for closing. Everything gets turned off. Everything. I make sure both Rob and I check."

"Elba, don't. They don't know where it started yet and even if it started in the restaurant, it could have been faulty wiring or...or anything." She had a hard time thinking of anything else it could have been. All she knew was Elba was losing everything, just like she was.

"Oh my God, my store!" An older woman tried to run past them, but Tim grabbed her around the waist.

"Ma'am, you can't go closer."

She struggled against Tim's hold as he tried to calm her down.

Zoe hadn't met her other neighbor yet. She'd been so busy getting the store ready she hadn't taken the time to walk next door to introduce herself.

Elba withdrew and stepped over to Tim and the woman. "Laura. You can't go closer. It's too dangerous."

She stopped struggling. "It's all I have," she whispered.

"I know." She hugged Laura and Tim let her go. Elba looked over Laura's shoulder at Zoe as Tim pulled her into his embrace. "I know."

Zoe stared at the flames devouring the building. It was all any of them had.

Tim turned onto their street and glanced at Zoe again. He'd taken every opportunity to look at her and check on her. She'd been almost silent for the last hour, barely responding with one-word answers. He parked in his driveway and turned off the engine.

"Are you—?"

She was already out of the truck, closing the door softly, and walking around the hood to go to her house.

He scrambled out. "Zoe. Talk to me." He caught up with her and tried to take her hand.

"Tim, I'm tired. I just want to go home and go to sleep."

She wouldn't look at him.

"Okay. I'm going to call into work—they'll understand."

"Alone."

She finally looked at him and it broke his heart. There was no life in her eyes. It could have been exhaustion but he could feel her pulling away, even though she was inches away from him.

"Zoe, it'll be okay."

"Exactly how is it going to be okay? How, Tim? Explain it to me. My entire life just went up in flames. Literally!"

"Insurance will cover—"

"The loan, if I'm lucky. It won't buy me new inventory. It won't find me a new location I can afford. It won't get me another loan and it sure as hell won't provide an income so I can live." She ticked off each item on her fingers.

"I'm here to help you."

"How? Are you going to support me while I figure out what the hell I'm going to do with my life?"

"If that's what you need, then yes."

"*Puta que pariu!*" She threw up her hands, turned away from him, and turned back. "I don't need you to take care of me, Tim. I don't need you to save me and I sure as hell am not going to rely on another man for anything."

She couldn't have shocked him more if she'd punched him. He inherently knew she was angry and lashing out, but that didn't make it hurt any less. "So I'm just another man now?"

He saw the shift in her gaze. The understanding that she'd hurt him, but she didn't answer his question and that hurt almost as much.

She shook her head and pressed her lips together. "I just need to be alone right now." She turned and walked away.

Fuck. He ran his hands through his hair and stared after her.

Following her would be a bad idea. Letting her walk away was a bad idea. He was well and truly fucked.

His phone rang and he pulled it from his back pocket. "Chief, I was going to call in a few minutes. I need today off."

"I need you in today. The fire downtown was arson."

"ELBA. THANK YOU FOR COMING IN." Tim ushered her into a conference room. "This is Chief Stewart, Drake Spencer, the fire department arson investigator, and Donald Fisher from Precision Security."

She waved nervously at the other three men as she sat. "This is about the fire?"

"Ms. Ballard, you recently installed a new security system through Precision Security, is that correct?" Drake asked.

"Yes." She glanced at Tim, then at Drake. Her answer was hesitant. He didn't blame her, but he'd agreed to let Drake lead the questioning.

"What was your reason for installing a security camera in the kitchen? It's not really usual for a small restaurant, is it?

She sighed. "No, but I want to expand into dinner service and serve wine and spirits. If I'm going to have—" She swallowed hard and cleared her throat. "If I was going to store alcohol, I wanted to make sure it was accounted for."

"And you chose to have the security footage maintained off-site on Precision Security's servers rather than have an internal recording system, is that correct?"

"Yes..."

"Was there a particular reason you chose not to have a system on-site to record the security footage?"

"Yeah. They make you rent the stupid recorder. It's a thousand dollars less expensive per year to have them keep the footage on their server." She leaned back in her chair. "What is this about? Did you figure out how the fire started?"

Instead of answering her, he pulled out several photos and spread them out in front of her. "Do you recognize the person in these photos?"

She leaned forward and stared at each photo and a furrow developed between her brows. "It looks like...it looks like George."

"George Baker, the building owner?"

"Yes. When was this taken?"

Drake pulled out a laptop, placed it in front of Elba, and pushed a button to play the video they'd all watched several times.

She watched as George moved around the kitchen of her restaurant, pouring cooking oil on the floor, turning on the stove, and throwing aerosol canisters into the ovens before turning those on as well. The video played for several more minutes before the oven exploded.

She jumped and yelped, covering her mouth with her hand and then looked at the men at the table.

"Why?" she whispered? "Why would he do that?"

"You don't know?" Chief Stewart asked.

"Why would I know? That restaurant—" She looked up and took a shaky breath. "He blew up my restaurant. He destroyed Zoe's bookstore. Laura's boutique. Why?"

ZOE DIDN'T WANT to answer the door. She wanted to wallow on her couch and be miserable, but the doorbell rang again. Just in case it was someone she wanted to avoid, not that she was actively avoiding anyone, she tip-toed to the door and peeked through the peephole, sighing when she saw Elba on the other side of the door. At least she would be able to commiserate.

She swung the door open and stepped aside to let her in. "Hey."

"Jeez, you look like shit." Elba didn't even bother with a side eye.

Zoe closed the door and threw the bolt. "I look like I feel. Margarita?"

"It's three in the afternoon."

"Life handed me a shitload of lemons. I'm putting them to use."

Elba followed her to the living room and took in the mess. "Have you left the couch in the last two days?"

"Yes," she said, plopping onto the couch in question. "I've gone to the kitchen for a refill and the bathroom for a defill. Is that a word? It should be a word. What brings you to *casa da miséria?*"

After removing a magazine from the chair, Elba sat down. "House of misery?"

"Yup. I think I'm entitled to a little wallowing."

"Yeah." She propped her feet on the coffee table and rested her head on her hands. "I came from the police station."

Zoe lowered her glass. "Why were you at the police station?"

"The fire started in the cafe. It was arson." She lowered her hand and picked at her nails.

She misheard. That was the only explanation. Who would set a fire in Elba's restaurant?

"What? Who? *Why?*"

"I don't know the why, but the who is George Baker." Her eyes were full of tears when she glanced up.

"George Baker the owner? Smarmy, sweaty, bad suit George Baker?"

"The same one."

"I don't— But why?"

Elba shook her head. "I don't know. They were issuing a warrant for his arrest when I left the station."

"Why did they call you into the station?"

"They showed me the video of George breaking into the

kitchen. Tim thought it was him, but he'd only met him once so he wasn't a hundred percent positive. They called me in to identify him. I think they also wanted to see if I had anything to do with the fire."

She shrugged and rolled her eyes, but Zoe could tell she was hurt by even the suspicion of having anything to do with it.

"Why the hell would they think you had anything to do with it?"

"They didn't say, but they asked a lot of questions about when the security cameras were installed and why I put them where I did. I guess they were thinking who would be stupid enough to start a fire when they knew there were security cameras."

Zoe's head dropped back and she closed her eyes briefly before tilting her head back up. "George didn't know we had the security systems installed—we didn't tell him. He didn't know there were cameras."

"Yup."

There was one silver lining. They knew who. Hopefully the police would be able to figure out why. Not that it mattered because their stores were a pile of burnt wood and ash.

Zoe looked at her half empty glass. Maybe it was too early for margaritas—she was downright maudlin.

Eh—she'd earned it. They'd earned it. She held her cup out to Elba and shook it, trying to tempt her best friend into joining her wallowing party.

Unfortunately, she shook her head. "April will be home from school soon and I need to drive home."

"Nonsense. Tell her to catch an Uber here. We'll be bad examples. Think of all the good it will do her when she goes off to college and people offer her alcohol. She'll remember that time her mom and Aunt Zoe were smashed and she'll be all, 'no thanks.' Really, when you think about it, we'd be doing her a favor."

Elba laughed through her nose at Zoe's convoluted reasoning. "I'm not going to be able to afford college."

Her laughter turned to tears. "What are we going to do?"

Zoe set her cup down and wedged herself into the chair with Elba.

"I don't know." She pressed her temple to Elba's. "We'll figure it out."

CHAPTER 27

Tim pushed up from the couch and kicked a beer can out of his path on the way to the door. He crouched to look through the peephole and swore under his breath. Shit. He'd forgotten Bree was coming by to pick up Mitzy.

He swung the door open. "Hey. Give me a few minutes, I need to get her things together."

Bree frowned and looked at him with concern. "Take your time. Jase is on a trip this weekend so I'm in no rush."

He scrubbed a hand through his hair. "I know, but I forgot you were coming today. Sorry."

"I can come back later if that's better."

"No. It'll only take me a few minutes."

"Okay." She closed the door behind her and followed him into the living room but stopped at the threshold. "Are you all right? Don't take this the wrong way, but you look like shit."

He glanced at her over his shoulder. "Long couple of days."

"Is this about the fire?"

"Some of it." He picked up the metal water bowl and carried it into the kitchen, pouring what was left in it into the sink and rinsing it out. He stacked it on top of the matching food dish and placed both into the plastic bin that held the dog food. All that was left was the bed and he'd finally be by himself. Again.

Fuck, that was a depressing thought. He'd gotten used to spending time with Zoe. That had been the hardest part of not seeing her for the last couple of days.

He missed her. But not enough to force himself somewhere he wasn't wanted.

"Tim?"

"What?" Bree had asked him something and he'd completely spaced. It wasn't like him to zone out like that.

"I asked if this was about Zoe."

"Yeah. I guess so."

Bree sat in the recliner next to the couch. "How is she doing?"

"Two days ago, she wasn't handling it so well."

"You haven't talked to her in two days?"

Fuck. Looked like it was therapy time. Jase had told him once that Bree was a good listener. Hell, maybe she'd have some words of wisdom for him on how to get over Zoe.

"You want a beer?" he asked. If he was going to bare his soul to his soon-to-be sister-in-law, he needed a beer.

"Sure."

He grabbed two longnecks from the fridge, popped the tops, and brought them back to the living room. Handing her one, he dropped into the corner of the couch closest to her and took a long pull from his bottle.

"So what happened?" she asked.

He picked at the label on the bottle and told her about the fire and discovering the building's owner was the one who set it.

"Do you know why he set it?"

"Probably the most fucked-up, selfish reason I could never even imagine."

Her eyebrows rose and she tilted her head, waiting for the reveal.

"He's getting a divorce and his wife was getting the building since she was able to show that she put up the initial down payment for it. He figured by starting the fire in the restaurant, it would look like an accident and he'd get the insurance money from the sale."

"Except he didn't know there were cameras in the restaurant," she guessed.

Tim shook his head. "They'd had them installed the week before. He had no clue."

"I'm guessing since it was arson the insurance company isn't going to pay out."

"Nope."

"Holy shit. Does Zoe know?"

"I don't know. I'm sure someone's told her."

"What do you mean you're sure someone has told her?"

"The morning after the fire, Zoe said she wanted to be alone and walked away. She hasn't answered any of my calls or my texts."

"Are you worried she'd hurt herself?"

He shook his head. "Mrs. Wilson, our neighbor, said she'd seen her and she was fine. Sad and depressed, but otherwise fine. That's the only reason I haven't busted down her door."

"But you want to bust down her door," she said.

"What's the point? It wouldn't do any more good than it did the first time I offered to help her. I told her I'd help support her until she figures out what to do, but she blew up at me. I'm not going to force myself on someone who doesn't need me."

"Now I see where Jase gets it. Your dad is like this too, isn't he?"

His brows furrowed. "Like what?"

"Super protective. Wanting to rush in and save the day and protect the damsel in distress."

"No. What's wrong with wanting to help the people you care about?" He silently turned the bottle in his hands for several heartbeats. "Is it really asking too much to be needed by someone?"

She didn't answer him directly. "Tim, do you think I need Jase?"

His head popped up. "What? No. I think he needs you more than you need him."

"He doesn't actually. He'd be fine without me. Maybe still living like a hermit, but he'd be fine." She shifted in her seat and leaned closer. "I'm going to let you in on a secret. Most people don't *need* anyone else. Especially strong, independent people." She paused. "I don't need Jase. I *want* him."

He shook his head. "I don't understand."

She sighed. "It's like a pair of shoes. I *need* shoes to protect my feet. I *want* a pair of gold, laser etched, platform, peep toe Christian Louboutin Privé heels, but I don't need them to protect my feet. It's the same with relationships. I don't need Jase—I'd be perfectly fine without him—but he's my version of those unicorn shoes. Thankfully sometimes life works out and you get what you want."

Out of all that, he understood feet and shoes. Everything in between needed an interpreter. "So I should figure out what kind of shoes Zoe likes?"

Bree chuckled. "Let me try another way. For women like Zoe —women like me—it's about the approach. If she thinks you're offering because you don't think she's capable of doing it herself, she's going to be insulted. She's smart, determined, independent, and can take care of herself. She doesn't need someone to do it for her."

"But she does. The bookstore is destroyed."

"Yes, her bookstore is destroyed, but she will figure out how to save herself." She paused as if weighing her words. "Strong, independent women don't *need* someone to fix our problems for us. We especially don't need a man to come in and rescue us from whatever life throws our way. What we *want* is someone who is able to stand beside us or even behind us and applaud our success. We want a partner. We want someone who we can share our problems with simply because we need to bitch about something. We don't need you to solve our problems for us—we just need to you listen to them.

"I hate to oversimplify it, but if you wouldn't make the offer to a guy friend...don't make the offer to Zoe." She leaned back and drank her beer.

The problem was, he would make the same offer to a guy friend.

He played that scenario out in his head and realized it wouldn't be the same. While he might offer to help Kevin in the same situation, he'd expect him to chip in for groceries and utilities and would expect him to find a job or a way to support himself. What he'd envisioned with Zoe was supporting her completely for as long as it took.

He scrubbed his hands through his hair. "So what do I do? Give her time?"

"Fuck no. If Jase had given me time when he fucked up, I'd have walked away. *Be* there. Tell her you're there. Don't let her forget that you're there. You're going to have to figure out what it will take for her to realize you're in it for the long haul."

He wasn't sure what he was going to do to make that happen or figure out how to be Zoe's unicorn shoes. Hell, he had a hard time even thinking "unicorn shoes."

"Jase said you were a good listener. He said people open up to you like they'd known you their entire lives."

She squinted her eyes at him. "Did he now?"

He sipped his beer. "Okay, what he actually said was it's a pain in the ass that complete strangers feel the need to share their life story with you, especially when you listen to the whole damn thing and then get invited to family dinners as if you've known those people your entire life."

"One time. That happened one time and the couple was very nice." She tilted her head. "You going to be okay?"

He gave her a half-hearted smile. "Eventually. As soon as I figure out how to be Zoe's unicorn shoes." He shook his head and stared up at the ceiling while sipping his beer. Unicorn shoes.

Bree smirked. "Telling her you love her is a good place to start."

CHAPTER 28

Zoe braced herself on the banister as she eased her way down the stairs on stiff legs while the percussion section of a marching band beat out a rhythm in her head. A three-day bender might have been a really bad idea. Bright sunlight streamed through the living room windows and made her head throb even more.

She stared at the mess of empty plates, glasses, and microwave meal containers strewn around her living room. The thought of smelling any residual alcohol in the glasses made her stomach roll.

Toast, ibuprofen, and water. Lots and lots of water. Dropping bread into the toaster, she filled the electric kettle so she could make some mint tea to help settle her stomach. A little bit of peanut butter on the toast would help as well.

The pity party was over. She'd needed to drown her sorrows and *not* think about her goals and dreams crashing in a literal fiery ball of flame. Now it was time to figure out what she was going to do. She needed a list.

Taking her plate and mug with her, she went to her office and stared at the poster board-sized pad that still had a checklist for the bookstore opening. She set the plate down and brushed off her hands.

Tearing the top sheet off, she started to crumple it but stopped and smoothed it out on her desk. She ran a hand down the list. She might need it again.

Maybe.

Whatever the future held, she still needed to deal with the immediate problems. She drew a small box, one she could put a check mark in, and wrote *Clean house* next to it.

Get copy of police/fire report

Call insurance company

Call bank

Her hand hovered over the page and she bit the inside of her mouth.

Apologize to Tim

She drew stars on either side of those three words with an arrow up the page, pointing above *Clean house*. Stepping back, she pursed her lips.

Tim was worth putting on a to-do list and he needed to be first.

Part of the reason she'd drunk so hard was because she kept seeing the hurt in his eyes when she'd lashed out at him. He'd only been trying to help. Deep down she'd known that, but when he'd made the offer so soon after the fire, all she heard was he didn't think she could handle it on her own. It had echoed all the doubts her family had spouted at her when she'd initially told them about her decision. She'd let her fear and her anger drive her reaction and it had hurt him.

"You're such an idiot," she whispered.

Hopefully it wasn't too late.

Returning her plate to the kitchen, she finished her tea and poured a large glass of cold water to take upstairs with her. Before she went anywhere, she needed a shower.

Thirty minutes later, feeling somewhat human, she pulled open the front door and scared the crap out of herself and Bree.

"Holy shit!" Bree flinched back a step and grabbed her chest. "Jesus. Sorry. That was unexpected."

"Just a little." Zoe's heart pounded in her chest. "I wasn't expecting anyone on the other side of the door."

"I wasn't either." She pointed inside. "Can I come in?"

"Um, I was actually—"

"It'll only take a few minutes."

Zoe sighed. "Sure." What was five more minutes before she had to grovel?

"Thanks." Bree followed her down the short hall into the living room. "Wow. Okay. Uh, do you need help cleaning up?"

"No. I wasn't in the mood to clean the last few days. I'll take care of it in a little while."

Bree turned around. "I heard about the fire. I'm so sorry. Let me know if there's anything I can do to help."

"Thank you for the offer. I'm not sure there's really anything anyone can do. Unless you happen to have a spare hundred and fifty grand lying around." Her laugh wasn't exactly humorous.

Bree cocked her head. "Why a hundred and fifty thousand?"

"That's about what it would take to refurbish a new location, purchase new inventory, and have enough solvency to operate for the first year." She pressed the palms of her hands into her brows and rubbed out. It made her head hurt just thinking about it. And her chest and her stomach. Her entire body rebelled at the idea of having to ask the bank for another loan.

She dropped her hands and caught the odd expression on Bree's face. She shouldn't have brought up money. It was one of those social norms she'd never understood.

"Anyway, that's probably not what you came by to talk about."

"Right." Bree shifted her weight and stood a little straighter. "It's about Tim."

Ooh. "Bree—"

"I know it's probably none of my business, but Tim is going to be family and he's a really good guy. He's one of the best."

"Bree—"

"I think you should give him another chance. He may come off as kind of controlling, but that's just him trying to take care of everyone. He's a protector. It's in his blood. Jase joined the Army and Tim joined the police force because he wants to protect those he—"

"Bree! I know. I was leaving to go apologize to him."

"Oh." Bree's shoulders sagged as if all the hot air had been let out of her.

"I didn't handle the situation well after the fire. I wanted to be alone and lick my wounds for a while and I kind of lashed out at Tim in the process. I know he meant well, but I— I just hope it's not too late."

Bree shook her head and gave her a lopsided smile. "I wouldn't be here if I thought it was too late."

"That's good to know," Zoe said. "So I'm going to go..." She raised her eyebrows and pointed at the door.

"Right! Sorry." Bree walked to the foyer and paused with her hand on the doorknob. "Listen, something else that probably isn't any of my business, but I have a couple of friends that work at the bank. If you want an introduction, I'm happy to help."

Zoe inhaled and exhaled some of her pride. She was going to need help. She couldn't do it all on her own this time and she needed to admit that, at least to herself. "Thank you. I may take you up on that offer. I need to make some calls first."

"I understand. Let me know. I don't want to lose the opportunity for a friends and family discount at a bookstore." She winked and let herself out the door.

Zoe waved as she got in her car, then looked over at Tim's house. His truck was in the drive which meant he was home. Which meant letting go of even more of her pride. More than help, she needed someone in her corner who believed in her.

And Tim did.

~

ZOE KNOCKED on the door and folded her arms. She uncrossed them and put her hands in her pockets. Her stomach rolled and she didn't know if it was residual alcohol or the fear that he wouldn't answer the door.

The handle turned and her stomach rolled again. Fear and nervousness then.

"Hey," he said.

"I'm sorry. About the other day. I was...I was a lot of things, but I shouldn't have taken it out on you. You were trying to help and I—"

His mouth on hers cut her off. His arms banded around her and lifted her onto her toes. She wrapped her arms around his neck and he picked her up and backed into his house.

The door slammed behind them as he set her back on her feet. His hands cradled her head and he eased off the kiss, dropping his forehead to hers.

"I'm sorry," he said.

"Why are you sorry?"

"For assuming you needed taking care of. For trying to swoop in and make everything better. I have a bad habit of thinking I know what's best for the people I care about." He lifted his head and stared into her eyes. "And I care about you very, very much, Zoe."

Jesus, her stomach. It didn't flip this much when she rode rollercoasters.

"I love you," he said. "I know it's only been a couple of months, but I've never been more sure of anything in my life. And I do want to take care of you. I want to protect you and support you."

He took a shaky breath. "I also know you're more than capable of accomplishing everything you set your mind to on your own, but I hope you'll let me help you."

She blinked several times. All she'd hoped for was *of course I forgive you*. This morning's hangover had brought more than a little clarity with it. In addition to the checklist of things to do for the bookstore, she had the knowledge that the reason missing Tim had hurt so much was because she loved him.

His returning the feeling was the last thing she'd hoped for.

"I know it may be too soon for you," he said. "You don't have to say it back. I'm good with you being here and giving me another chance."

"*Euteamo.*" It came out in one quick breath, forced out by her desire for him to know she felt the same way.

"*Eu te amo?*" he repeated.

"I said it in Portuguese?"

He grinned, displaying his dimples to their full effect. "You did."

"It means I love you," she said.

"Thank God." He dropped his mouth to hers, his tongue sweeping in to stroke.

She didn't know it was possible to sigh and gasp at the same time, but she was fairly certain she did.

He spoke between kisses. "I promise…I'll try not to interfere. I'll wait…for you…to ask…before I offer help."

"I want your help, Tim. But you're right—I don't want you to take care of things for me. Just be there." She kissed him the same way he'd kissed her. "As a sounding board. Listen to my problems without trying to solve them for me."

He smiled against her mouth. "That's almost exactly what Bree said."

She pulled her head back and frowned. "Bree?"

"Yeah. She came by for Mitzy and ended up giving me a kick in the ass. I was trying to figure out how to get you to talk to me when you showed up."

That interfering matchmaker. She smiled. She might have already made the decision to apologize to Tim on her own, but she appreciated Bree's dedication. "I hope she gave you some good advice."

"The best." His hands traveled down her neck and shoulders, his thumbs brushing against the outside of her breasts.

A trail of goosebumps followed in the wake of his hands, down her torso to her waist, before ending up at her hips.

"I don't know if you have plans," he said. "But if you're free, I have some ideas for how to spend the rest of the day."

"Does it involve exploring the width of your bed?"

"You're very perceptive, Ms. Acevedo."

She checked her watch. The bank closed at two o'clock on Saturdays. Screw it. They'd be open first thing on Monday. "Turns out I have the weekend free."

"Funny. I feel a fever coming on. I might have to call in sick tomorrow."

She loved his affinity for elastic-waisted gym shorts. She ran her thumbs between the waistband and his skin. "I do know some basic first aid. I should probably stick around and make sure it's not too serious."

He smirked. "That sounds like a good plan to me."

"The best."

CHAPTER 29

S ummer had finally given way to fall, just in time for Jase and Bree's wedding. Red and gold leaves created the perfect backdrop for the ceremony and reception, as if special ordered from the florist. Bree had been nonchalant about the entire thing. Tim had spent the last couple of weeks reining in Jase as he turned into groomzilla, demanding everything be perfect for Bree, even though she only cared that it didn't rain and there was plenty of wine and beer.

Thankfully, autumn turned up full force ten days before the big day, as if knowing to do otherwise was inviting Jase's wrath.

Now Tim stood next to him under a canopy of fall colors, listening to his brother choke out his vows. He was going to give him so much shit later. He glanced at Zoe sitting in the second row and winked. She grinned back at him.

The last two months had been hard for him, watching Zoe struggle as she fought with the insurance company and the bank...and her family. He'd wanted to jump in and knock over every obstacle that presented itself. His restraint had been rewarded when Zoe had asked for his advice on how to address certain issues and he found he enjoyed discussing possible ways of resolving problems. Zoe looked at things from an entirely different perspective. She didn't always agree with his suggestions but was always willing to talk through them with him. He learned he didn't always have the best answer.

Almost a month after the fire Zoe, Elba, and Laura were notified that the building had a new owner. One who was willing to not only rebuild but also renovate to their individual specifications. The salon owner had chosen not to re-sign a lease and Elba had decided to incorporate the extra storefront into her restaurant. The lease offer had been more than generous. Everything was handled through a lawyer and the owner remained anonymous.

Tim glanced at Bree as she repeated her vows. He had his suspicions, but unless she wanted to come clean, he'd keep her secret.

A cheer went up when Bree and Jase exchanged their first kiss as bride and groom. Tim laughed and clapped when Jase pumped a fist in the air, still kissing Bree. They finally broke apart and Bree took her flowers from Denise. She kicked up one gold-clad foot and raised her bouquet in the air before Jase tucked her hand into the crook his arm and led her down the aisle right as the sun dipped below the horizon. It might have been timed better if Jase hadn't been so busy mauling his new bride.

Tim stepped forward and offered his arm to Denise and they followed Bree and Jase. He gave Chris a head nod as they passed and Denise blew him a kiss. They'd already planned for Chris to escort Zoe to the reception while they took care of signing the marriage certificate and taking photos.

"Are you going to ask her today?" Jase asked.

Tim glanced away from Bree and Denise, holding on to each other while they laughed hysterically as the photographer tried to take photos of them together.

"Ask who what?"

Jase gave him a look like he was an idiot. "Ask Zoe to marry you."

"If I was going to ask Zoe to marry me, and I'm not saying we're at that point, it sure as hell wouldn't be at your wedding."

"Why not?"

"Bro, seriously? How long have you lived with Bree? You don't steal the limelight from the bride."

"Bree's not going to care."

"Regardless, I'm not to ask Zoe to marry me today. I kind of need to work on getting on her family's good side before I pop the question. They weren't too happy when I told them they weren't welcome in my house if they were going to continue yelling at Zoe and making her miserable."

Jase grinned at him. "Seriously?"

"Hell, yes. Her sister made her angry cry. I'd had enough. Told them to get out and not come back until they could support her decisions."

"How'd that go over with Zoe?"

"Eh. She yelled at me in Portuguese, so not all that great."

Jase laughed and slapped him on the shoulder. The ladies finished with their pictures and joined them and Jase took the opportunity to kiss his new bride.

"Well, this is awkward," Denise said.

"Right? You'd think they'd have gotten over this by now."

Jase flipped them off but didn't stop kissing Bree.

"Aren't you guys supposed to make a grand entrance or something?" Denise asked.

The happy couple finally broke apart. Bree sighed. "If we have to."

"Told you Vegas was a better idea," Denise said. "But noooo, you wanted a big wedding. Forgot about the big reception that goes along with it, didn't you?"

"Why do I keep you around?" Bree asked.

Denise grinned at her. "You love me."

Bree frowned. "I should have made you wear an ugly dress."

"Whatever. Let's go. The sooner you make your entrance, the sooner you can go find the honeymoon suite."

Tim shook his head and followed her as she walked around to the where the caterer had set up a large tent for the outdoor reception. "Not an image I needed in my head."

"Hey, at least I kept it PG."

He only had time to give Zoe a quick kiss on the way to the reception. Between dinner, greeting family and friends, and the toasts, it wasn't until the music started that he finally had a more than a minute to spend any time quality with her.

Pulling her in close, his hand drifted down her bare back to her waist. "Have I told you how much I like this dress?"

She grinned up at him. "A couple of times when I was trying to get you out of the house on time."

He smirked. "There's a reason they call it a quickie, you know."

"I think your definition of a quickie differs from everyone else's since I always end up at least thirty minutes late whenever I let you talk me into one."

"If you gave in faster, we'd have more time."

"If we moved in together maybe we wouldn't need them as often," she said.

He stopped dancing. "What?"

"Mom and Dad want to buy a condo in Fort Lauderdale. Selling the house will let them buy the condo without incurring a new mortgage." She shrugged and dropped her gaze. "Unless it's too soon."

Tilting her head back, he kissed her. "It's definitely not too soon. It's damn near perfect."

Her smile was blinding. "I think you're perfect," she whispered.

He shook his head. "I'm only perfect with you."

EPILOGUE

*Z*oe closed her eyes and rested her hands on her stomach, feeling her breaths as she inhaled and exhaled. It was happening. Again. Hopefully it would stick this time.

No more fires. No more crazy landlords—although she didn't actually know who her landlord was, so there was always the possibility that he or she could be crazy. She took it as a good sign that a company was handling everything, though.

"Zoe. You okay?"

She opened her eyes and smiled. Tim stood in front of her with an arm resting on one of the bookshelves while he looked at her with concern.

"Yes. Just trying to keep from having an anxiety attack."

He pulled her into his arms, wrapping them around her. "You want me to cause a commotion while run you out the back?"

She pressed her temple into the pocket of his shoulder and chuckled. "No. I only needed a few minutes to take a deep breath. I feel like I've been going non-stop for the past six months."

"That's because you have been." He rested his head on top of hers. "It's going to be great. You've got this."

She did have this, but it still felt good to hear it from someone else—especially from Tim. He'd been there every step of the way, letting her vent about timelines and contractors, and offering her advice and encouragement. He'd propped her up when she needed it and made her take a break when she didn't think she needed to. He'd been everything she hadn't known she needed and more.

"Thank you." She lifted her head from his chest and craned her neck back to look at him. "I don't think I would have gotten through this without you."

"I've seen your checklists, remember? You'd have been fine."

"Maybe, but I don't think I would have been as sane."

"Who said you were sane now?"

She poked him in the ribs. "Jerk."

Tim smirked and flinched to the side. "You ready to stop procrastinating? Elba's looking for you."

"Why didn't you tell me that to begin with?" She pushed against his hips so he'd let her go.

"You looked like you needed a hug," he said.

"You just wanted to feel me up." Zoe turned and walked between the bookcases toward the side of the store.

"Maybe..."

His voice was filled with amusement and she glared at him over her shoulder. She found Elba opening the large, folding doors that separated the bookstore from the Cafe

"Hey. You ready?" She slid the last of the panels into the wall recess.

"As ready as I can be," Zoe said. "You?"

Elba rested her hands on her hips. "Absolutely. Let's do this."

Zoe wished they had a complicated hand-shake high-five they could do, but neither of them knew one and she wasn't coordinated enough to come up with it on the spot.

"See you on the other side," she said.

"I'll have the wine ready," Elba replied.

The crowd was considerably larger than the first time she'd

opened the doors to the bookstore, but she and Elba had heavily advertised the grand re-openings of both the Cafe and the bookstore. She was glad she had scheduled all the clerks she had hired, including the part-timers.

She'd seen Bree and Denise in the restaurant while helping a customer find a book so it was no surprise when they entered the bookstore from that direction.

"Zoe, it's gorgeous!" Bree hugged her. "I love what you and Elba did with the space. It feels very old-world Europe."

Zoe smiled. "Thanks. We went round and round with the architect the owner hired on how to transition between the two areas so that it felt like one cohesive space, but were still two separate stores."

"I'm glad you went with the folding doors instead of the gate," Bree said.

Zoe cocked her head. "How did you know we discussed putting a gate in?"

For a second, Bree looked panicked. "Um...Tim must have mentioned it to Jase."

Zoe might have believed her if it hadn't been for the hesitation in her voice and because, "I never mentioned the gate to Tim. Elba only talked about it once and neither of us liked the idea."

Denise looked anywhere but at Zoe or Bree, even going as far as glancing at her empty wrist.

"Bree...are you the owner?" Zoe asked.

"Yes! I bought the building. It's a good investment and it helped out a couple of friends." She leaned forward and braced her hands on her knees, then straightened and rested them on her hips. "Whew. So glad the cat's out of the bag. It was killing me."

Denise shook her head. "How did you ever get a clearance? You suck at keeping secrets."

Bree shot her a withering look. "Shut up. I didn't want to keep this secret."

Zoe flung her arms around Bree's neck. "Thank you. I don't

know why you thought you had to keep it a secret, but thank you, thank you, thank you. I promise you won't regret it. We'll be perfect tenants and we'll make sure it stays a good investment."

She hugged Zoe back. "Tim was worried you wouldn't accept the terms of the offer if you knew they were coming from me."

"You know, he was probably right. Now I don't care." She let go of Bree and looked at Denise.

"No offense, but I'm not a big hugger," she said.

"None taken," Zoe said.

Bree leaned close. "I'll get her for you later."

Denise rolled her eyes. "God, I hate you people."

Bree shook her head and mouthed, "She loves us."

"I'm leaving." She turned away but called over her shoulder, "Zoe, your store's awesome."

Zoe grinned. She'd spent enough time with Bree and Denise the last few months not to be offended by Denise's brusqueness.

Around two in the afternoon, the crowd began to thin and gave everyone a chance to relax a little. So far they hadn't faced any major issues other than running out of a couple of the most popular children's books, but she'd issued IOUs to the customers with promises of a discount on future purchase. All-in-all, not a bad problem to have.

"Zoe."

Zoe looked up from the tablet she was checking inventory on and found her mom and step-father on the other side of the counter. "*Mamãe?* How—? What are you doing here?"

She set down the tablet and walked around the counter to hug her parents.

"Tim called us and told us about the grand opening. Why didn't you tell us?"

"*Mamãe*, you haven't supported me this entire time. I honestly didn't think you'd be interested."

"Oh, *querida*. Of course we're interested. We love you."

Brian, her step-father, wrapped an arm around her shoulders.

"We're very proud of you. Your mother and I are sorry you've doubted that—we only want the best for you."

The backs of her eyes stung. Her mom had apologized for telling Mark where Zoe was staying, explaining she thought Zoe had still been in love with him, but it had been hard feeling like she couldn't talk to them about what was going on with the bookstore.

Her mom hugged her tight and Zoe squeezed her eyes shut as her familiar scent surrounded her. Letting her go, she wiped at the moisture under her eyes.

"Would you like a tour?" she asked.

"We'd love one," her mom said.

Hours later, she climbed the stairs to her and Tim's bedroom. They'd finally moved in together two months ago when her parents had found a buyer for the house, and she still had to pinch herself sometimes that everything was so perfect.

Pushing into the bedroom, she paused on the threshold. "Cheating on me already?"

Tim grinned. "She's keeping my feet warm."

"When are you going to admit you don't want to give her up?" She sat on the edge of the bed and scratched Mitzy behind the ears.

"I already told Denise you'd fallen in love with her and couldn't bear to see her go."

"Of course you did. She's going to have to move if you want me in bed with you."

"I have something for you." He leaned around her and rummaged in the nightstand. Sitting back against his pillows, he held out whatever he'd retrieved from the drawer.

Zoe blinked at the small gold ring between his thumb and forefinger as the deep green emerald sparkled in the light from the lamp.

"That's my grandmother's ring."

He tilted it toward him, then back at her. "Yes."

She looked at him in shock. "Where did you get my grand-mother's ring?"

"Your mom brought it with her. She said it was your favorite when you were a little girl."

"It was." She was having a hard time catching her breath. Was he doing what she thought he was doing?

Tim sat up. "Zoe Mariana Olivera Acevedo, will you marry me?"

Meu Deus. "Yes," she whispered. "Yes!"

He slid the ring onto her shaking hand. "I love you."

Zoe pressed her lips to his. "I love you."

He smirked against her lips. "You remember when you were stuck in that window?"

"Yes..."

"I have this fantasy..."

The End

ACKNOWLEDGMENTS

As always, there is a whole list of people I want to thank.

My children who are just beginning to understand what it means when Mommy says, "Let me finish this paragraph."

My sister for inspiring the frappuccino scene in the market. Yes, it really happened. Yes, she handed me the cup and walked away. It wasn't as bad as I made it in the book. Also, there wasn't a hot cop standing behind me when I turned around.

Elisabete - thank you for being the inspiration for Zoe, for not giving me too much grief for not remembering any of my Portuguese from twenty-six years ago, and for answering every "How do you say?"

Elba - for coming up with the most popular title.

My fantastic editor, Jessica for your guidance, feedback, and always amusing comments.

Kelley - Thank you for jumping into this series at the very end. For giving me the focus I was lacking. I can't wait to see what we can do next.

Lori - Wow! Thank you for my beautiful, gorgeous, drool worthy covers!

Eric - your photos are always beautiful. Good luck on wherever life takes you next. I, for one, am sad to see you go but I'm so happy to have me you and I can't wait for #LAYBOMAE2020!

As always, you the reader. Whether you're in my FB reader group, in the A2T2 reader group, or randomly found this book and gave it, and me, a chance. I wouldn't be able to do this without your continued support.

Thank you. Thank you. Thank you.

Happy Reading.

ALSO BY TARINA DEATON

The Combat Hearts Series

Stitched Up Heart

Half-Broke Heart

Locked-Down Heart

Rescued Heart

Holiday Heart (only available to newsletter subscribers)

Coming Soon

The Jilted Duet

ABOUT THE AUTHOR

Tarina has spent her entire life in and around the military - first as a dependent and then as an enlisted Air Force member.

In 2015, a friend challenged her to complete NaNoWriMo. She dusted off one of the many stories she had started over the years, threw it in the trash, and started all over.

Tarina is still active duty and a single mom of six-year-old twins. Her favorite hobby is sleep. She has delusions of retiring from the military and being a stay-at-home mom.

You can connect with Tarina at www.tarinadeaton.com and email her at tarina.deaton@tarinadeaton.com.

facebook.com/tarinadeatonauthor

twitter.com/tarinadeaton

instagram.com/tarinadeaton

bookbub.com/authors/tarina-deaton